# Risking Immortality

## Alyson Root

Interior formatting and cover design by:

Tara Sullivan,The Write Gal Co.

www.thewritegal.com

*If there is one thing I am sure of,*
*I am sure you have always belonged with me.*

-Akif Kichloo

# One

Today is my twenty-ninth birthday. To so many, this year is insignificant. But to me it signifies an inevitability, one I have been desperately running from since I was born; a truth I am woefully unprepared to handle. The reality that one year from now, when the sun sets, I will be forever changed. My thirtieth year will mark either the start of my immortal life as a mated vampire, or my spiral into madness.

Before I go on, I think it is important to explain the origin of my kind. The truth, not the fabrications spewed by humans for millennia. First, vampires are born, not made. I have a mother and a father. I also have seven siblings. We are carried in the womb and born in the same manner as a human baby.

Second, we are creatures of light, not darkness. However, we are forced into the shadows by the lies told by a species frightened of anything "different." A species that has vilified us because they are too ignorant to learn and accept our differences.

Third, we do have elongated upper canines—"fangs" as humans like to refer to them. However, they are not retractable, and they are not two inches long. In fact, unless you were really looking, the slight differences between vampire and human teeth are hardly noticeable.

The canines are a leftover evolutionary facet. In the early days of creation, vampires had to hunt their own food. Just like those of gorillas or big cats, elongated canines helped them take down their prey. We have no need for such things now.

Vampires walk among you. Since the first human evolved, there has been a vampire right beside them. Many stories and mythologies paint us as the devil's spawn, born from darkness and evil. Another flagrant lie. Vampires are simply a different species, evolved with a different genetic code.

The sunlight does not scorch our flesh; we do not burst into flames at the sight of a cross. Hallowed ground is sacred to our kind just as much as humans. We live and love, but we *are* cursed. Humans got that right.

Our elders would frown at the term I use. To use the word *cursed* implies something more than what it is—a simple glitch of nature. Unlike humans, a vampire must have mated by the end of day on their thirtieth birthday. I don't mean in the physical sense. A vampire must find their mate, their other half. Why? We do not know. Vampires have spent countless years searching for the answer, but it eludes us still. Our knowledge is based on the results of thousands of years witnessing the poor, unfortunate souls that were unable to find their match in time.

Humans have depicted vampires as blood-sucking animals. I will admit, there is a degree of truth to it. But what the human world fails to explain is why a fraction of our species behaves in such a way. Let me enlighten you.

As the sun rises on a vampire's thirtieth birthday, a cellular change begins. If that vampire has found their true love, their immortality is guaranteed. Destined to live for thousands of years in bliss alongside their mate.

However, if the vampire begins this change without their soulmate, the process is corrupted. Instead of bliss, the vampire descends into madness, craving human blood with an insatiable thirst. Those are the vampires etched frighteningly into the human psyche. Laughable really when you examine the history of humanity and the countless bloody wars they waged in the name of power and greed. For us, it is unavoidable. Our choice is taken from us the moment the sun sets on our birthday. Of the two species, who are the real monsters?

Another by-product of our condition—that's how it should be defined, I think; if it's not a curse, it is a condition, and one that must have an answer—is our fertility. The only way vampires can bear children is if they are mated. A vampire can sleep with the world's population before they change and no pregnancy will occur. It is an impossibility. Thankfully, our condition does not discriminate against those of us who are attracted to their own sex. Our community helps same-sex couples find surrogates and sperm donors. We celebrate life and often have large families. Although that isn't a given. Each vampire couple determines if they wish to be parents or not. Which wasn't always easy before birth control. A vampiric invention, I might add.

Another glaring difference between humans and vampires, don't you think?

My kind works together, celebrating love in its purest form, no matter how that may look. Humans ostracize, discriminate and persecute their own kind because one woman may love another. Shame is brought upon families because a man fell in love with another man. Again, I ask you, who are the monsters?

It is my dislike of humans that fuels my desire to keep a distance from them. My parents wish for me to interact with humans. They feel we should embrace them, teach them about our kind. Come out! I wholeheartedly disagree with their beliefs. Why try to teach them about our kind? Humans don't even want to learn about their own species.

"Happy birthday, Amelia." My eldest brother Laurence perches on the end of my bed. Oh, yes, we sleep in beds. Not coffins. Although, it is fun to play up the stereotype at Halloween. Inside jokes and all that.

"Good morning." What I am least looking forward to today is the worry on the faces of my family. Every member of the Loch family found their mate, except the youngest. All of them before their twenty-fifth birthday. I am the last but one of our family and I am no closer to finding love now than when I was as a young vampire.

"Brought you breakfast," Laurence says, handing me a plate of pancakes and a mug of type A. Yes, we drink blood, we have to. Our blood requirement is the same as a human's need for water. But—and this is a big but—we do not feed on humans. We do not hunt them... Only the unmated are responsible for those kinds of behaviors. Those of us under thirty and those who are mated drink only animal blood. The taste of human blood is repulsive. It doesn't sit well in our stomachs.

"Thank you." I take breakfast and begin eating. Laurence sits there watching me. I know he wants to speak of the coming year. Over the past six months, he has tried in vain to get me to talk about my upcoming birthday and what it means for me.

"Amelia, we need to talk."

"About?"

"Playing dumb doesn't suit you." Laurence shifts a little closer. He is a handsome male. Tall, closing on six-foot-five, thick dark hair, perfectly styled. Our family is blessed with good physical genetics. We all have good looks. It's not my ego talking, it's the truth. We are a family of raven-haired beauties.

"Laurence, there isn't anything to discuss. I have a whole year to find my mate, otherwise I will go insane. There. Topic covered. Can I eat my breakfast in peace now?"

"Why are you taking this so lightly, sister?"

"How else should I take it? Be realistic Laurence. It's unlikely I'm going to find *the one*. All the family, including our youngest cousins, matched well before their thirtieth birthday. Julien found his mate at sixteen. I am the odd one out, the blip on the family's immaculate record. Instead of worrying about me finding a mate, I suggest you worry about which one of you has to take me out." I'm not being dramatic or fatalistic, but realistic. There is no point ignoring the obvious. I am an anomaly in the Loch family.

"Do not let Mother and Father hear you speak of such things, Amelia." Marcus, the second eldest, marches in with a severe face. He has been listening at my door. This is why I dread coming home to stay. Everyone gets far too comfortable in everyone else's business.

"Marcus, you must see that I'm right?" Marcus is a realist like me. If anyone should see my point of view, it's him.

"I understand your point of view." Marcus earns a scowl from Laurence. "But I don't think you have given it your all to find someone."

"I agree," Laurence barks.

"I go out. I socialize. No one has pinged my interest."

"When was the last time you went out, Amelia? Hm? I'll tell you when. Three months ago, for my wedding anniversary."

He's right, of course. I'm not the type of woman to go out on a Friday night. Well, not every Friday night. Not when I have a good book waiting for me in the comfort of my own home.

"Laurence is right. Staying in with your books is okay *after* you have found your mate. Now is the time to be scouring the land. I will not lose you, Amelia." Marcus has a fire burning in his eyes. I can feel the fear radiating from him... the fear of losing me to madness, the fear of watching as I become unhinged.

I have been awake for ten minutes, and already I want the day to be over. Laurence and Marcus are just the beginning. My other siblings will be on the same mission. As for my parents, I know they will have plans in place. I expect to be set up on multiple dates.

"Amelia, you own three bars and two nightclubs. Why on Earth aren't you frequenting them, looking for your woman?"

"First, I have four bars and three nightclubs. Second, they are all unfortunately overrun with humans. Not so good for me. Third, I have staff who manage and run those establishments, meaning I don't have to go there."

"They are not *overrun* with humans. You're just bitter that Mother wouldn't allow you to make your establishments vamp-exclusive." Laurence rolls his eyes at me.

"Do you blame me?" I feel indignation course through my veins. Humans offer us nothing but pain and suffering. Of course, the general population of humans is unaware of our existence, but there are few among them that hunt us down. Believing in the bile spewed by uninformed hypocrites. Claiming to do the Lord's work. It makes me sick. What's so wrong with me wanting to stay away from them? Be amongst my kind, safe?

"Vampires aren't saints, Amelia." Laurence laughs mirthlessly.

"I'm not saying we are."

"We're getting off topic," Marcus growls. Out of all my siblings, Marcus is the one I am closest to. "You have to start trying harder. Whether or not humans are there."

"Fine, I'll go out. I'll visit my bars and clubs." I don't have the energy to fight them. A drink in each place should suffice. Prove to them it's a futile exercise. "Can you go now, so I can dress?" Neither brother looks satisfied with my answer, but it's the only one they will receive.

"Fine, we'll meet you downstairs, but Amelia... this conversation is not over." Laurence warns.

As soon as they are gone, I flop back down to my bed. I want nothing more than to close my blinds, hike up my duvet and sleep the day away. My desire is rudely ripped from me, as are my covers. Lucille, my sister, stands glaring at me. We are usually the more combatant family members. Lucille is the opposite of me. Where I like quiet and comfort, she likes noise and turbulence. Lucille loves humans—I do not. She has them rotating in and out of her bed daily. The thought makes me gag.

"Get up," she orders. I have lost count of the physical altercations I have had with Lucille. Although I can be the calm to her storm, I am no pushover. When things get heated between us, there is usually a wake of damage left behind.

Vampires have a couple of traits that bear a resemblance to the stories crafted over time. Our physical strength is elevated. We can't lift cars or bend metal, but we are slightly stronger and faster than our human counterparts. Our vision is generally better, too. "If you leave, I will dress," I hiss.

"You have five minutes, then I'm coming back up here and dragging you downstairs. The entire family is waiting for you."

It's my twenty-ninth birthday, the day the clock begins its countdown to my impending fall into madness.

# Two

The breakfast with my family is going as well as I imagined. When I first sat down, I got the perfunctory Happy Birthdays, which lasted all of thirty seconds before the hard-hitting questions. Mainly from my parents.

Harlan and Victoria Loch are formidable people. They have walked the Earth for over two hundred years. They caused quite a stir when they mated, by refusing to procreate immediately. Instead, they took their time traveling the world, gaining skills in a myriad of sectors. That is why the Loch family is the third richest vampire family in existence. Only the Grand Master and his brother outrank us.

When they finally birthed a child, Harlan and Victoria became dedicated parents. We wanted for nothing. They showered us with love and affection. All of us are successful in our own rights, thanks to their tutelage.

It seems, though, that I am now letting the family down. Distress and frustration are rife between us. My parents want a plan of action. They cannot fathom why I haven't made more of an effort to find my true love.

Perhaps they are right. Surely there should be a sense of urgency overwhelming me, but there isn't. It's possible I have accepted my fate. After my twenty-fifth birthday passed, it was as if something in me cracked. Any hope I once had faded. It's possible that not all of us are destined to find our soulmates. There has to be a reason, I'm sure. That's when I decided to simply live my life. Every member of my family may find my inaction frustrating. They may think I am willingly wasting my life by reading at home. It doesn't matter. There is nothing I can do to change the outcome.

If it were as simple as an arranged marriage, I would have done it, but love is about free will and that internal fire that is stoked by the other half of a person. Love can never be feigned or coerced. Let's be realistic, the planet has nearly eight billion people on it. I think anyone who successfully finds their mate is beyond lucky.

"Amelia, my love, please, you must make more of an effort." Victoria, my mother pleads. It's as if she thinks I'm being difficult on purpose.

"Mother, I cannot force a match," I hiss. I have endured breakfast for half an hour and my usual calm is waning. Do they not realize that every time they pester, it is a vivid reminder of what will become of me?

"Amelia, please don't speak to your mother that way." Harlan, my father, interrupts. I get my quiet calmness from him.

"Sorry, Mother." I take a few calming breaths. "Laurence and Marcus have already raked me over the coals—"

"We did not," Laurence interjects. "We were simply stating what needed to be stated. You have to make an effort, Amelia. There is a mate out there, if you would only look a little harder."

"And as I said in my bedroom, I will make the effort."

"Yes, you will," Lucille barks, "tonight, in fact."

"Oh, are we having a night out?" Maria asks. She is the second youngest child. She and Lucas, the baby of the family, are close. Maria found her mate last year. A delightful vampire called Mitch. His family is respectable, and he loves Maria. That's all I need to know about him.

"Yes, we are," Lucille answers. "Tonight, the Loch siblings are out for blood," she cackles. I roll my eyes. Lucille loves drama.

"Surely I should have a say about where and what I wish to do on my birthday."

"Last year, yes. This year no. You've wasted too much time and now we are intervening," Lucille replies, a devilish glint in her eyes.

"It's a good idea, Amelia," my mother adds. I will not win this fight. I nod in acceptance. How I wished I'd stayed in my room with the pancakes Laurence brought me.

"That's settled then," my father comments. "Time for birthday gifts."

I smile gratefully, even though I want for nothing. My parents always give lavish gifts. I've had more cars than I can count. A house and expensive jewelry. In reality, my tastes are much simpler, but I won't let on to them, not when their faces light up so brightly when they get a chance to spoil one of their children.

This year's gift is a vacation to Hawaii. I've been several times already, and I love it there. For once, I'm glad they went all out. A break from the constant chatter will be a godsend. A full year of listening to each member of the Loch family harp on about my final months as a sane vampire is enough to send me over the edge before I turn thirty.

"Thank you, really, this is perfect." I kiss both my parents.

"It's open-ended so you can go when you please. Hopefully with a woman," my father winks. I grin, but it's fake. I will be going to Hawaii alone; I have no doubt.

"We all got you a new bike," Aliah, sibling number four, chimes.

"A bike?"

"Yes, a Ducati."

"It cost a fortune, so you better use it," Lucille adds. There is always a tinge of anger in her words, especially when directed at me.

"Of course I will. In fact, I think I'll take it out this morning." My love of motorbikes comes from my mother. I have loved every single bike she has owned, even the ones I was too young to remember. There is an entire room dedicated to her passion in the house. I remember spending hours in there with her, poring over old photographs. Most of her machines are displayed in a garage she had specifically designed as a showroom.

"Maybe I'll tag along," my mother adds. I smile widely for the first time today. Spending some quality time riding my bike with my mother is the best birthday gift I could ask for.

The rest of breakfast passes cordially. My family has finally stopped talking about finding a mate. Well, at least for now. I know this evening will be about my siblings throwing women at me, left, right, and center. Not that I'm going to complain. I won't find my mate, but I might get a birthday fuck out of it.

The day is bright and warm, as is the norm in California. I take my time studying my new Ducati. It is beautiful.

Matte gray with black trim. My siblings chose well. I'm not the kind of woman who likes flashy colors. My tastes must come from my mother in that department too. Her Yamaha pulls up alongside me. She's dressed in all black like me. Her bike is dark blue with black trim. I chuckle to myself because we fit the human stereotype for vampires. Long dark hair, rather pale skin and clad from head to toe in black.

"Ready?" Mother asks. I place my helmet over my head, taking one last look at my new bike before straddling it. There is nothing like the feeling of 168 hp between your thighs to make you feel alive.

We pull off and my heart soars. I can feel the power beneath me, ready to be unleashed. But until we hit the coastal roads, I have to restrain myself. As we join the Pacific Coast Highway, I feel my body itch with anticipation. We can't speed unreasonably, but we can let go a little. As if my mother has read my mind, she opens the throttle and takes off. I smile and follow suit. The ocean shimmers beneath the sun, reflecting like diamonds on a blue velvet bed. This is the best way to spend my birthday. Cruising along, forgetting about the doom and gloom that awaits me.

We have been riding for roughly an hour. Time means nothing to me, though, not only because vampires have more of it than most, but because pure joy cannot be caged by time. In this moment of euphoria, linear timelines dissolve into nothingness. I am one with my bike.

The lights and sirens of a police car interrupt my bliss. Instinctively, I check my speed. Yes, I'm a little over, but not by much. Sighing, I follow my mother, indicating and pulling over to the side of the road.

Taking my helmet off, I slowly climb off my bike and prepare my license. I know exactly who has pulled us over and I find myself amused. Officer Dana Brooks is a forty-year-old-looking vampire that I have had a few fun nights with. You might wonder how that works, seeing as she must have found her mate. Dana found her mate when she was sixteen. Dana and David are polyamorous. But no matter how many others they invite into their bed, they are soulmates.

The male of the species has never attracted me, so thankfully I got a one-on-one experience with Dana, sans David. It was a good time. My mother has also dismounted and removed her helmet. "Dana, good to see you," she calls as Dana approaches. They hug. The vampire community is a tight-knit group. Nearly everyone knows everyone.

"Victoria, you look beautiful as ever." Dana is an incorrigible flirt.

"As do you, Dana."

Dana turns to me with a wicked smile. "Happy Birthday, Amelia." Her embrace is tight, and she squeezes my ass. I laugh because she is terrible.

"Thank you. Is that why you pulled us over, to wish me a happy birthday?"

"Yes, actually, although you were pushing the limit back there."

"Only a little," I pout.

"Hm. Well, I'll let you off this time," she says before moving closer to me, so her mouth is just by my ear, "Only if you let me get you off later?"

My mother has taken a few steps away, seemingly interested in the ocean below us. "Are you going out tonight?"

"Maria invited me to your birthday bar crawl."

"Then yes, I'd say there is a fine chance you will be getting me off."

"Excellent," she purrs and then bites my earlobe. "I'll let you be on your way. Have a fun ride and please try to stick to the speed limit." Her warning is soft but directed at both my mother and me. I'm not the only speed freak in the family.

We decide to turn back and head home. If it were up to me, I'd continue until we hit San Francisco, but alas, I have a birthday to get back to. The return journey is not as relaxing. All my thoughts turn to tonight's festivities. Instead of having a fun night with my family, I'm going to be thrown in the middle of their meddling. Despite my repeated explanations that a match cannot be forced, they persist in their attempts to make it happen.

The house is a hive of activity when we pull up. Laurence and Marcus are playing with their children in the pool. Aliah, Maria and Lucille are sitting on the patio drinking, discussing which club we should go to first. Lucas and Jacob are in the kitchen cooking an early dinner for us all. My father is poring over papers laid out on the dining table. Considering they are in separate areas of the house; the Loch family makes a racket.

"Come on," my mother urges. "Let's go say hello." She knows I want to go to the library and hide away amongst the books.

"Fine," I mutter. I'll have all the time in the world when I get home to read. Well, all the time that three hundred and sixty-five days provides. After that, my reading time will be the last thing on my mind.

# Three

The limo ride to Insomnia is a loud affair. My siblings are known to go a little crazy, and tonight is no exception. Insomnia is the biggest club I own, spanning several floors. Maybe you can guess from the name that it operates until the sun rises. It's been a few months since I have visited, mainly because Insomnia attracts hordes of humans.

The champagne is flowing and I'm happy to acquiesce. If I'm to survive tonight, I will need liquid courage. We all topped up on Red before we left the house. Red is how we refer to blood. Lucille is in fine form. Sadly, she left her husband at home to babysit. Trent is a lovely man, with whom I get along rather well. It baffles me as to why he finds Lucille attractive. Not physically, but emotionally. Her character is... well, I think he deserves better, but once again, it's not my choice or theirs. They mated, and that's that. He turns a blind eye to her revolving door of human bedmates. Trent loves Lucille and their son Benjamin. For him, that's enough.

Lucas turned twenty-one last month, so this is his first official outing. I'd prefer to celebrate that than my birthday. He looks overly excited, which makes me smile. Lucas is a kind soul. I might be closest to Marcus, but Lucas is the one I think will resemble me, personality wise. He reads and writes. More often than not, when I call him, he is in his library. Lucas has yet to find a mate, but he has nearly a decade. I'm not worried.

Maybe I should be worried by the amount of alcohol he is consuming at an alarmingly fast rate. "Will you stop worrying?" Marcus laughs. "Tonight is about fun. Lucas will be fine, and so will you if you just let go a little."

"He's going to be ill if he doesn't slow down."

"So what? That's his choice. Amelia, please try to enjoy tonight."

"Easier said than done, Marcus, especially when you all start throwing me to the wolves."

"Throwing you to the wolves?" Aliah laughs. "Amelia, women are not wolves."

"Some bite." I wink, causing everyone to laugh.

"Well, maybe that's what you need. Anyway, yes, of course, we are going to be on the prowl, but I promise, the most important thing for all of us tonight is that you enjoy yourself and celebrate your birthday."

"Fine, let's party." A loud cheer echoes through the limo. I can't help but laugh. I love my family, even when they infuriate me.

The driver comes to a stop outside Insomnia. There is a line around the corner which makes me happy. Usually when I stop by my clubs and bars, I park around the back and discreetly enter that way. Not tonight, though. Oh, no, the Loch family have arrived in style.

I see patrons straining to get a look at the people in the obnoxiously large and flashy limousine. Our family is well known among humans. We have our hands in many things. I'm sure to them we are just entitled assholes. They aren't privy to the centuries of work it took my parents to get us where we are today.

Lance the door man greets us enthusiastically. I like to think I treat the staff well. I know them all by name and I am aware of their personal lives. The majority of people who work in my clubs and bars are vampires. There are a few humans, too. I leave the managers to do the hiring and firing, unless I feel the need to intervene.

The club is thumping and I'm certain it's almost to capacity. We deposit ourselves in the VIP section. There are bottles of champagne in metal buckets on the tables. Lucille is already opening one. She's going to be trouble tonight; I can feel it.

In the distance, I see Claire, the club manager, making her way over. She is tall and slim with raven colored hair, similar to mine. Hers falls in waves though, whereas mine is pin straight. We've known each other for years, and when I opened Insomnia, she was the only option to run the place, in my eyes.

"Happy birthday, boss," Claire laughs, pulling me in for an embrace.

"Thanks. How is everything?"

"Perfect. The club is the number one place to be."

"Excellent. Any issues?"

"Amelia, it's your night out, not a work meeting."

"I'm just asking." I'm not just asking. I was hoping Claire could distract me from the sudden nervous energy that has sprung up in my stomach.

"Okay, I'll give you a quick rundown. I fired Todd and hired Erin."

"Todd, he was a recent hire. What happened?"

"Caught him banging a patron in the storeroom."

"You did well." All employees know that engaging in sexual activity with a patron is off limits. "And this Erin?"

"She's twenty-seven, has worked in bars and clubs since college. Her cocktails are excellent, and she is a hard worker."

"Sounds like the perfect replacement."

"Now, back to the party," Claire laughs. "I'll get some more drinks sent over."

Half of my siblings are on the dance floor, making some questionable moves. I forget sometimes that Laurence and Marcus are closing in on forty (as far as humans are concerned, anyway). The aging process may stop at thirty, but it can take a little time, which gives us some leeway. After that, we rely on humanity's vanity. In fact, humans make it too easy sometimes. Half of Hollywood strives to remain ageless. Plus, filters. That was one of our better inventions. You're welcome.

Even though they have stopped aging, it seems their characters are still hurtling towards middle age. Lucille has already latched on to some poor human. I hope he has health insurance. Lucas is still sitting in the booth, looking a little green.

"Drink this," I say, pushing over a bottle of water. He takes it and sips it gingerly. He is going to feel like death in the morning. I swallow down my champagne and decide to hit the dance floor. I might as well enjoy myself.

Thankfully, I wore a light black bodysuit. The swarm of bodies is making the temperature soar. I weave my way through the crowd, trying to reach my brothers. I see the looks of want from more than a few men and women as I pass. None of them pique my interest. I can smell they are human.

My body reacts instantly to the bass. I move and let the music run through me. Now and then I feel a brave soul try their luck by dancing close to my back. I move away without interacting. I know I come across as a cold bitch, but I don't want to spend all night explaining why I don't welcome their advances.

Sweat is dripping down my forehead. I've been dancing nonstop for a while. My brothers are still in the dad dancing zone, so I head to the bar. The crowd is three deep, even with three bartenders.

Being the owner has its advantages, like slipping behind the bar to serve myself. I'm just bending down to one of the under-counter fridges when I feel a presence behind me. I catch their scent, which momentarily makes me freeze. It's not a scent I have encountered before. It's sweet like cherries. Not the usual smell of either a vampire or human.

Before I can stand up to see who the mystery person is, they bark at me. "What the hell do you think you're doing?"

I stand up straight and turn around. The woman looks incensed, her eyes are shimmering with anger. "I'm getting a drink," I reply calmly.

"I can see that. Surely you aren't stupid enough to think you can just nip back here and help yourself. What kind of bars do you usually go to?"

My amusement must show on my face because she visibly reacts by straightening herself to her maximum height. Which isn't terribly impressive, if I'm honest. I'd say she hits five-foot-four, maximum. And yet, even though I tower over her, she still postures. I want to laugh. This woman clearly has no idea who I am. "I rarely go to bars," I answer. She looks confused.

"Maybe that explains this then," she says, waving her hand between me and the fridge. I take a moment to look at her fully. She's dressed in the bar's signature black shirt and trousers. Her hair is tied into a high ponytail. The golden hues shine under the many strobe lights. Her eyes are piercing blue. And, without sounding too lecherous, her tits are amazing. Even hidden underneath the shirt, I can tell she has a pair of tantalizing assets.

"I'm not sure why you're getting so upset," I say casually. Cracking open the water bottle and taking a sip. Fire burns in her eyes.

"Are you fucking kidding me?" she explodes. Her outburst turns me on. "You don't work here, dumbass. You can't just saunter back here and help yourself."

I don't think I've ever been called a dumbass to my face before. It's quite refreshing, and funny. I then remember the conversation I had with Claire. The firecracker in front of me must be the new hire, Erin. I smile at her before stepping past and making my way back to the VIP area. I can feel her eyes burning holes in the back of my head.

"What was that about?" Aliah asks. I turn to look back at the bar and sure enough, Erin is still standing ramrod straight, shooting daggers at me. I chuckle and turn away.

"That's the new bartender."

"You looked like you were arguing."

"Nope, she just wanted to know why I was back there grabbing water."

"Why would she want to know that?"

"Because she has absolutely no idea who I am."

"Oh shit, what did she say when you told her? Fuck, I bet she was mortified," Aliah laughs.

"I didn't tell her," I grin.

"Oh, you're mean."

"Well, she didn't ask, so…"

We're interrupted by a white piece of paper being slammed onto the table. Looking up, I see Erin, who is standing there scowling. I look at the item she nearly put through the table. It's a bill for the water. I can't help the laugh that I release. Reaching into my purse, I pull out a fifty-dollar bill and hand it over. "Keep the change," I say. Her scowl deepens as does my laugh. She storms away and I lose sight of her.

"You are so mean," Aliah cackles. That was the first genuine bit of fun I've had with a woman in a long time. I don't have long to mull over what occurred because Dana arrives. She's wearing a dress that could be classed as a belt and I know it's for my benefit.

"There you are. Come on, let's dance."

We head back into the fray. Our bodies meld together, and I know for certain I will take her to bed tonight, or to the table, possibly on the couch. Wherever we decide, it's going to be fun. Dana is adventurous, and she's not afraid to ask for what she desires.

Even though we are surrounded by hundreds of people, I am still acutely aware of Erin. It's like I can feel her presence, which is strange. Without looking, I can pinpoint her. The memory of her scent clouds my mind. Such a sweet and inviting smell. But that's not what I'm thinking about. I'm wondering why I have never come across someone with that scent. Vampires and humans all have the same underlying scent that distinguishes us. It doesn't matter which perfume or cologne is worn; the scent of a species is always the same. But not Erin.

I'm pulled out of my fog by Dana cupping me. She's tired of dancing and wants to take the party elsewhere. I have a penthouse apartment above the club, which will suffice. Grabbing her hand, I lead her to the back of the dancefloor. A panel conceals a set of stairs. It's bio locked, so only I have access.

We head upstairs, but before I lose sight of the room, I shoot one last look over at the bar. Erin is busy serving. She's graceful and efficient. My heart stutters, and then Erin looks up. Our eyes meet and I see the look of confusion on her face. I wink and pull the panel closed.

For now, I need to put Erin to the back of my mind. Dana is ready to help me celebrate my birthday and I need what she's offering.

# Four

I wake up alone, which isn't surprising. Dana likes to have her fun and then leave as soon as possible. It doesn't bother me. I prefer mornings to myself. Normally I sit on my balcony with a cup of coffee, watching the city come alive. Since staying with my parents, I haven't had the chance to have a morning to myself, not with so many siblings loitering around. I swear none of them, except Lucas, understands the need for peace and quiet.

Thankfully, my apartment above Insomnia is kept fully stocked and cleaned. I never know when I will need to use the place. Not that I stay here regularly. Like I said, it's been months since I last visited.

Stretching reminds me of all the acrobatic sex I had last night. Dana put me through my paces. My legs ache as much as my pussy. Hell, everything aches.

I make my way over to the kitchen on wobbly legs. The penthouse is an open concept. Everything in the kitchen is top of the line. It came that way when I bought the building. I like new things but the sterile chrome and white isn't my style, I just haven't bothered to decorate it to my taste. What's the point when it's more like a hotel room than a home?

Once my coffee is brewed, I head to the balcony. I don't bother with clothes; I'm too far up and frankly, I don't care who sees me. The morning sun is already hot, showing another glorious day.

Sipping my coffee, I recall yesterday. I replay the conversations with my family over and over. Maybe they are right, and I haven't been putting in the effort to find my mate. I always believed my mate would find *me* if I'm honest. I romanticized everything, and when I realized that wasn't how my story was being written, I...what? Gave up? *Have I given up?*

The result of not being mated isn't lost on me. I know my family believe I'm being too laid back but in reality I'm terrified. No vampire wants to end up unmated. My thoughts wander to last night and to Erin. Her mystery scent is still puzzling to me. The way I could track her movements also causes distress, but I'm not sure why.

Insomnia will open at nine this evening. There is a cocktail hour before the DJ arrives. I wonder if Erin will be working again. Maybe I should introduce myself? I'm secretly looking forward to seeing her face when she realizes who I am.

That still leaves me with the rest of the day. I should head back to my parents, but I'm enjoying the solitude. I'll stay here for a little longer. It would actually be a good idea to go over some work things while I'm here. Claire takes care of everything, but she knows I like to be kept in the loop.

After a satisfying shower, I can walk properly again. Dana really went at it last night. I take the stairs back down to the club and make my way to the office. The silence is inviting. When I first bought the place, I often wandered around the rooms when it was closed. I would make myself a drink and lounge around, taking it all in. Maybe I'll have myself a drink by the bar after I have gone through the finances.

As usual, Claire has left the office immaculate. She is organized and efficient. I never have any problem finding what I need.

As I thought, the profit margins are excellent. I couldn't ask for better. Maybe I could look into opening another club. A sister club to Insomnia. New York maybe?

Time has passed quicker than I thought, and I have to get back to my parents. My mother will throw a fit if I just disappear on them. The drive back takes less than fifteen minutes. Like yesterday, the house is full of people and noise. Before I endure the onslaught of questions, I run to my room and change into a bikini. I may as well lounge by the pool for a few hours.

"There you are!" my mother shouts when I stroll over to her lounger.

"Here I am," I reply.

"I thought you would have been home hours ago."

I suppress my eye-roll. I haven't called my parents' house home for years. "I stayed at the club to get some work done."

"It wouldn't hurt to take a few days off, Amelia. Maybe that's why you haven't found your mate."

"Yes, paperwork is the reason," I mutter. "You know, it's not my fault, right?"

"What do you mean?" Mother raises her sunglasses to her head, her eyes lock on to me. I don't know where my emotions are coming from, but I'm suddenly pissed that my family is constantly making me feel like it's my fault I haven't found a match. Like I warrant the future that lies ahead of me.

"I've looked, Mother, I've been out. I know you all think I sit around doing fuck all in my library and sometimes, on an evening, that's exactly what I do. But not all the time. It's not my fault I haven't found her, so will you all stop making me feel like a fucking failure! I get it. I'm the disappointment and I'm sorry that one of you will have to put me down, but it's not my doing." My voice has risen and I'm panting. I can feel the blood rushing through my ears. Where this sudden outburst has come from, I don't know. What I do know is that I need to leave.

Turning on my heel, I run back inside, ignoring a blur of shocked faces as I go. Sprinting upstairs, I change into my leathers and run to my bike. Nothing and no one is going to stop me. Turning the throttle, I wheel spin out of my parents' garage.

My mind is racing. Is the madness already starting? I'm the calm daughter, the rational, reasonable one. Not the child that acts in anger or with vats of emotion. Is this it? Am I seeing what will happen to me? Will I decline from now on?

I kick up my speed, tearing through the streets until I hit the 101. I don't give a shit about the speed limit now. I'm determined to outrun my spiraling mental state.

I couldn't tell you how many hours pass. Eventually, though, my mind and my speed reduce to a safe level. The sun is setting, and I know I have to go back.

As I pull into the garage, I see my mother leaning against her Yamaha. We remain silent as I park the bike next to hers. Taking my helmet off, I struggle to look in her eyes. "Where did you go?" she eventually asks.

"Nowhere in particular," I answer. We grow silent again. I take a chance and look up. Her eyes are soft and understanding. They are also marred with fear.

"My darling, I... we never meant to make you feel you were failing us. Your father and I never want you to think that. Do you understand?"

I nod but find it impossible to answer with words. My throat feels raw.

"We're just scared, honey. I'm sorry that has come across as blame-shifting. We just love you so much and the thought..." Her voice cracks and I move to take her into my arms. The reality of the situation is that the Loch family is scared. Holding her tight, I let my tears fall. I might be a realist, but I'm still a person. A vampire that doesn't want my life to end in one year. That doesn't want to put my loved ones through that kind of pain.

We hold each other until our tears have dried. Taking my hand, Mother guides me back into the house. The dining table is set, and all my siblings are sitting waiting, along with my father. "I'm sorry honey," he whispers as he hugs me.

"We don't blame you," Laurence adds. "We're just scared."

"I know. I'm sorry for getting so worked up. I don't know what that was."

"It was natural, sis," Lucas says. "I don't think any of us realized how much pressure we were putting on you."

"I'm still setting you up," Lucille calls from the far end of the table. I roll my eyes, but for once I don't feel she is being antagonistic.

"We're here for you, Amelia," Marcus whispers in my ear as I sit next to him. I squeeze his hand in a silent thanks.

The chatter breaks off into individual conversations, which makes me feel better. I'd prefer a mundane chit chat rather than another round of "woe is me, I'm going to die soon" type of conversation.

"Hey, did you tell that new bartender who you were?" Aliah asks, amused. The table grows quiet, and I can see the questions on their faces. I laugh and recount what happened with Erin.

"Oh my, she sounds feisty," my mother laughs. That's one way to describe Erin. She's definitely feisty.

"I'm going to stop by this evening and introduce myself," I say. It's on the tip of my tongue to mention that strange scent I got from her, but something makes me hold back. Maybe I'd drunk too much, and it distorted my senses. I'll find out this evening.

It's almost nine by the time I excuse myself from the table. This evening's attire is a black cocktail dress. It's not too fancy but makes me feel sexy. I pair it with three-inch heels and some simple eye make-up. My hair is in a high ponytail, and I know I look damn good.

Insomnia is relatively busy by the time I arrive. It's still very early for a club, but I'm happy to see there is a decent crowd at the bar. Deciding I want a few minutes to observe Erin, I lower myself onto a bar stool at the far end. I have a clear line of sight and I like what I see.

Erin is still as graceful as she was last night. However, tonight she is less fire and brimstone and more earthly paradise. She's laughing with Kit, our other bartender. Kit has been in my employ for seven years, at least.

They work together well. My eyes wander over the crowd at the bar, and, to no surprise, Erin has more than a few admirers. One guy in particular seems taken with her. He's handsome if you're into that kind of thing. I wonder if Erin is. So far, she has remained completely professional with him. He has tried to buy her a drink three times in the few minutes I have been sitting watching. Each time she blows him off without being rude. She has more patience than I do.

Claire enters the bar from the office, and I slink farther back into the shadows. I don't want to be spotted just yet. Claire, Erin and Kit share a laugh about something. There is a great working dynamic between them all.

Mr. Pushy leans over and touches Erin's arm. Her eyes flash with anger. It's the first sign of that feisty woman I met last night shining through, and I like it. She takes a step back, regards him, and then leans forward, whispering something in his ear. Mr. Pushy pales and sits back, scratches his neck and then promptly leaves. I want more than anything to know what Erin said to him.

Claire approaches her, and they speak for a second. Now they are laughing again. A spike of something shoots through my chest. It's a feeling I'm unfamiliar with and that makes me feel uneasy.

I square my shoulders and shuffle over slightly so that I'm in the light. It's time to find out about Erin.

# Five

The moment Erin spots me, I want to break out in laughter. The airy fun Erin disappears in a flash and the angry hellion appears once more. I wonder what she is going to do. Will she try to evict me? Maybe call security?

"At least you figured out which side of the bar you should be on," Erin snaps as soon as she lands in front of me.

"It's not too busy this evening, so I don't mind waiting to be served this time." I know I should put an end to the games, but she's too much fun to play with. Plus, I want some time to... okay, this will sound creepy, but I need to smell her.

Cherries. She still smells like cherries. How is that possible? Who is this woman, and how the hell am I supposed to find out if she's a vampire or a human? Claire must know, surely. Yes, I'll ask her. Now, I'll continue to irritate my new playmate.

"If I see you approach this side of the bar again, I'll have you thrown out. Do you understand?"

"My, my, you are a feisty one. What's so special about your bar?"

"Listen, lady. You might dress fancy and think you are God almighty, but when you step into this club, you are a customer. Do you know what could happen if you had an accident? Insomnia is insured for workers only. You do not step behind this bar. Please don't make me call security on you this evening."

Wow, I'm wet. This woman is all kinds of hot when she's on her high horse. Holding up my hand in a scout's honor, I promise not to go behind the bar ever again. "Can I have a glass of water, please?"

"Water? That's all you want?"

"Yes, please." Watching Erin walk away is a lovely sight to behold. Claire has spotted me and wanders over.

"Wow, twice in twenty-four hours. What's the occasion?" I know the game is up now. I can't continue playing with Claire hovering, so I decide she should be the one to let the cat out of the bag. Erin returns with my glass of water. She is looking between me and Claire, obviously trying to work out what's happening.

"Thanks, Erin," I say when she sets the water down.

"How do you know my name?" She asks. I smile. Claire is looking confused.

"Of course she knows your name. Amelia knows every employee."

"Oh, so you're a regular?" Erin asks innocently.

"Erin, Amelia is the owner."

"No, she's not."

I burst out laughing at Erin's indignation. The mere thought that I, the pain in the ass customer who has riled her up to perfection could be the owner of this fine establishment is unthinkable.

"Erin!" Claire admonishes.

"Claire, it's fine. I've been playing with her a little."

"Oh, Amelia," Claire whines.

"I'm sorry. Erin, that goes for you, too. Please let me introduce myself properly." I extend my hand. "I'm Amelia Loch."

"Erin Hanson," she replies robotically.

"I'm sorry, but how the hell did this happen?" Claire asks, so I recount our meeting last night.

"Shit, Erin, that's on me. I should have introduced you. We were just slammed."

"No, it's on me. I'm sorry, Ms. Hanson, really."

Erin is clearly torn between wanting to tear me a new asshole and being a respectful employee. I kind of feel bad now. "It was nice to meet you, Ms. Loch. I need to get back to work, please excuse me."

"Oh shit, she's pissed," Claire laughs.

"I was only playing. I didn't mean to make her that angry."

"Erin is a tough nut to crack. She doesn't take shit, and she doesn't enjoy being made to look a fool."

"What should I do?" Suddenly, making Erin happy again is the most important thing for me to do.

"Nothing, she'll cool off. Anyway, it's not like you'll be around here much longer." The barb stings. Claire is a brilliant manager, and she's my friend. I haven't been a very good one of those recently.

"I know. I'm a shitty friend. Forgive me?"

Claire rolls her eyes. "Obviously."

"Hey, by the way..." My voice trails off because I'm not sure I should ask my next question, but I need to know. "Is Erin a vamp?"

Claire furrows her eyebrows and stares at me like I'm stupid. "No, of course not. Can't you smell her?"

Shit! Erin is human. And I couldn't tell. Oh, fuck, it's starting already. I'm changing. "I..."

"Amelia, you couldn't smell the difference?" Claire's eyes betray her concern.

Looking from Claire over to Erin, I weigh up how much I should say. "I... she smells different."

"What do you mean?" Claire whispers, leaning closer to me.

"She smells of cherries."

Anyone would think I'd just taken a swing at Claire the way she reels back, her eyes bugging out her skull. What the hell did I say?

"Amelia..."

"What?" I'm panicking now. Does Claire think I'm already starting to fall into madness?

"We need to go. Come on."

She leaves no time for a reply. Claire scurries off, speaks to Erin before rounding the bar and grabbing me forcefully by the elbow.

"Claire, what the fuck?" I protest, but it falls on deaf ears. Claire is on a mission. I'm stuffed into the back of her car. Claire tells her driver to take me to my parents' house. That's when I know my fears are coming true. For whatever reason, my descent into crazy town is being accelerated.

My head is pounding, and I can't organize my thoughts to produce a coherent sentence. Claire has tapped her heel the entire journey and I'm about ready to tear her leg off but thankfully we arrive, and she whips open the car door dragging me out.

My parents look equally shocked as I do when Claire tears into their home, calling for the Loch family to gather. My siblings must hear the panic in Claire's voice because they all come running. We are standing in the kitchen and I'm pretty sure I'm going to vomit.

Should I tell them to put me down now? That would be best for everyone. Do the deed before I become something they don't recognize.

"Amelia, repeat what you said," Claire barks.

"About what?"

"Erin?"

"What about her?"

"Tell them what she smells like?"

"Cherries?" I answer, and there is an audible gasp. "What, what did I say?"

My mother rushes over and grabs my shoulders tightly. Her eyes are boring into me. "You smelled cherries?"

"Yes, why?"

"Are you sure?" my father asks.

"I know what cherries smell like."

"It could have been her perfume," Marcus adds.

"Unlikely, you know our scents can't be masked like that," Laurence says.

"What the hell are you all talking about?" I practically shout.

"Amelia," my mother starts. "You've found her!"

"Found who?" I can't process what they are saying.

"Your mate, dumbass," Lucille shouts.

"No, you're wrong," I say with certainty.

"We're not wrong," Father replies.

"You could be," Claire interrupts because, like me, Claire knows something they don't. Erin is a human, and vampires cannot mate with humans.

"What aren't you telling us?" Jacob asks.

"Erin is a human," I say.

The silence that falls is deafening. My mother and father share a look, but it's not the one I expected. I thought, for sure, they would regard me and then each other with sadness. My chance, slipping through my fingers, but that's not what is happening.

The thing about being married for a couple hundred years is the ability to talk without using words. They've always had the ability to know what the other is thinking, and it is infuriating. Now more than ever.

"Why are you doing that weird, silent conversation thing?" Lucille asks, and I actually chuckle.

"Everyone sit," my father calls. We follow his demand and take our usual seats around the table. Claire sits on Maria's knee. They're close friends too, so it's not weird. "Amelia, this is going to sound..."

"Unbelievable," my mother finishes.

"Okay." I have no idea where this conversation is going.

"There have been a few cases of vampire-human mating."

"Gross," I mumble.

Mother ignores my childish outburst and continues. "Each time the... the vampire still fell into madness."

"Wonderful," I laugh mirthlessly. Basically, what I am being told is that my stupid body has mated with a species that is incapable of fulfilling what I need to become immortal.

"There are stories," my father begins. "Stories that tell of a vampire, ages ago, who mated with a human successfully."

"And are those stories based on truth or legend?" Marcus asks.

"We don't know," Father answers.

"So let's get this straight," Lucille interrupts. "Amelia has found her mate, but it's likely she will still turn nuts."

"Lucille," Mother snaps.

"No, she's right. If all the vampires who mated with a human still turned, I think it's time to face the truth. I know we're all scared, but this pretty much seals the deal, right? In twelve months, one of you will have to kill me."

Another collective gasp. I'm too numb to react to my own words. Probably because the truth is finally sinking in, and I have to be okay with it. For their sakes as much as my own.

"It is not a foregone conclusion," Aliah says forcefully. "We need more information. There is too much speculation to know completely."

"Aliah is right. We will look into it. In the meantime, you, Amelia, need to get better acquainted with your mate."

"She's not my mate," I reply through gritted teeth. "She's human."

"Oh Lord," Lucille laughs. "Amelia, don't be thick. Your dislike of humans is ridiculous. Let it go. So some of them hate us, big fucking deal. Most of them have no clue we exist."

"And how, dear sister, do you think Erin is going to react to that? Hm? Oh hi, Erin, I'm your soulmate and a vampire. Care to get hitched?"

"Moron," Lucille hisses. "Obviously, it will take time. The situation needs to be handled with delicacy, but it's not impossible. The only thing in your way is you."

Our tempers are flaring as they usually do. I'm ready to launch myself across the table and beat the shit out of her. Fighting Lucille feels like a good plan to me. I know it's not right, and it's definitely childish, but she irks me, and I need an outlet for all this pent-up rage.

"Will you calm down!" My father's booming voice cuts through the din. We all fall silent, just like when we were kids, and pushed him too far. "Thank you. Now, I know this is a lot, honey. But please, Amelia, see it for the miracle it is. You have found your mate. This time yesterday, each one of us feared the worst. But we have hope. And we have a full year to figure this out."

Once again, in my selfishness, I forgot how my parents would feel. Yes, I'm slightly horrified I have mated with a human, but on the other end of that is the light. The fact that I'm not broken or different from my family. It's also given them the hope that I will be okay. I mean, not completely, because let's be real. The odds don't seem to be in my favor, but they are better than they were yesterday.

"Another slight hiccup," Claire chimes in, and I know what she's about to say.

"Now what?" Maria asks.

"Well, Erin isn't exactly Amelia's number one fan."

"Is she even into women?" Lucas asks. Good question really.

"Yes, she is, but after what Amelia pulled, I'm not sure she will be into her."

"She's the bartender you teased?" Laurence sighs.

I stifle a laugh because it's still funny. If only they could see how cute Erin is when she's all fired up.

"Okay, the first job on the list is to get Erin to like you."

"Ugh, hard task. I've known her all my life and I don't like her yet," Lucille deadpans. Yeah, I'm going to kick her ass.

# Six

Considering I was only supposed to stay with my parents for my birthday and the day after, I'm a little shocked to still find myself here a week later. Ever since I smelled fucking cherries, my family has become obsessive.

My parents have spent every free hour talking to our elders and reading books. My siblings have been concocting ways to break the news to Erin that vampires exist. I have to say that Lucille's idea is my favorite. Wait until Halloween, do the whole vampire family dress up thing and then casually drink the blood of a squirrel in front of her. Of course, Erin would just think we were a bunch of lunatics, but it would be funny.

For my sins, I have been trying my hardest to wrap my head around everything. The idea of loving a human repulses me because I know what they are capable of. What if sweet Erin turns out to be one of those assholes who believe vampires are a virus that needs wiping out? I could be exposing my family to danger. None of them have thought about that, though. Oh no, they are all on the train to Erinville. They think she is my savior, whereas I'm scared she's my ruin.

Claire has been spending a lot of time at my parents' home, trying to help in any way she can. It's been nice to connect with her again. I hadn't realized how isolated I'd become until this week. Clearly, I had already resigned myself to a brief existence because I'd effectively pushed away friends and family. So, maybe I'm less of a realist and more of a frightened child?

Tonight, I have decided to visit Insomnia again. Claire has provided me with Erin's schedule. I need to see her again to figure out if she really is my mate. I'm struggling to come to terms with it. Yes, I felt something that night. Her no bullshit attitude was a major turn on, but being horny doesn't mean we are destined to be together.

My parents spent a little time describing what it felt like for them. As did a couple of my siblings. Apparently, they all smelled fruit when they bonded with their mate. My mother described the same ability to track my father's presence without looking, just like I had felt that night with Erin.

There is no doubt now that my body recognized Erin as being the other half of my soul. It's my mind that cannot accept it. Another glaring problem is that each vampire is always looking for their other half. Erin isn't, well, not that I know of. She has no reason to think I'm someone special to her. There is no guarantee she will ever feel anything towards me. Well, maybe anger. She displayed that emotion in abundance. What I'm saying is that Erin has no stake in this. Vampires' bodies are wired to search for their missing piece. There has never been an instance where a vampire has been rejected by their mate. Erin could easily reject me.

With so much going on, I need to take a step back before I see her. My eyes need to be wide open for this to be a possibility. I have to connect with her and see if it's reciprocated. If it is, and that's a big if, I need to woo her. If I'd mated with a vampire, our bond would have solidified the moment we came together physically. For vampires to fulfill the mating need, they have to give themselves to each other emotionally and physically.

Lucille described in great detail how she did that with her husband. I wanted to bleach my entire body after hearing it, but it gave me some insight. Lucille and Trent met at a bar and were in bed together the same night. That's how fast they cemented their bond. Both of them told me how they knew they were each other's mate and that the thought of not being with each other was unfathomable from the moment they bonded.

It is going to be more of an uphill battle for me.

To win that battle, I need a strategy. Erin spends most of her time working, so it stands to reason Insomnia is where I need to be. Instead of moving back to my home, which is an hour away, I intend to move into the penthouse suite above the club for the foreseeable future.

Claire was more than happy for me to take over the running of Insomnia for a little while, especially because it meant she will have the opportunity to travel to my other establishments.

Instead of dressing for a night out, I slip into form-fitting black slacks, a white pinstripe shirt, and a black waistcoat. The impression I left on Erin was less than ideal, and I need to turn it around. None of my family notice me leaving. They are so wrapped up in plotting and researching.

To release some anxiety, I take my father's Aston Martin. A car isn't as fun as a motorbike, but the roar of the DBS is enough to elicit the same thrill. Cruising to the club takes less time than I'd hoped. Pulling around the back, I hand the keys to my private valet. The glint of excitement in his eyes as he regards the DBS is almost comical.

Slipping in through the back allows me a few extra seconds to compose myself. Tonight, I must be in business mode. I want Erin to see the real me, but that won't happen until she has shed our past encounters.

There are still a couple of hours to go until the club opens. The bar is silent, so I take my time reacquainting myself with the area. With a glass of ice water in hand, I stroll between the tables, my eyes roaming every inch of space. Claire has done a fantastic job of running Insomnia. So well, in fact, I may ask her to continue traveling around my other venues, advising and managing on a full-time basis.

Losing myself in work is easy, even though it has been a while since I committed myself to running one of my clubs. I fall into it easily again. The hours tick by unnoticed until a sharp rap on the office door snaps me out of my fully immersive profit-and-loss world.

"Come," I call, my eyes still scanning the documents in front of me. The door opens almost silently. It's only the small gasp that makes me look up into the startled blue eyes of Erin.

"Ms. Hanson, what can I do for you?"

"What are you doing here?" she blurts, and I try my hardest to smother a grin. "Shit, I'm sorry, that was rude. Good evening, Ms. Loch."

"It's fine. I don't blame you. Actually, I'm glad you're here. Take a seat." She does as instructed. Her face is pinched, but she's not radiating white hot anger, so that's a step in the right direction. "And please, call me Amelia. None of my employees call me Ms. Loch."

"Sure, Amelia. Call me Erin then."

"Wonderful. Okay, so I want to clear the air. I owe you an apology for the first time we met. It was my birthday and even though I was far from drunk, I'd had a couple of glasses of champagne and was feeling a little playful. I certainly didn't mean to make you feel deceived or foolish. Please accept my sincere apology." There, that was from the heart. Surely, she can't still be mad after that.

"Thank you and I accept. Looking back, I know I came at you a little aggressively. It's just that I take work seriously and I know Insomnia has a stellar reputation. It's the reason I agreed to work here. When I saw you behind the bar, I panicked. All I could think of were the many, *many* health and safety violations being broken."

"And I thank you for that. I want all my employees to take their job and this club as seriously as you do. So, can we start again?"

"Of course, Amelia, with pleasure."

My belly flip flops when Erin speaks my name. The scent of cherries intensifies, and I have to take a beat to rein in my feelings. Feelings I'm not sure how to interpret. "Claire tells me you are an excellent bartender. I haven't had the time to peruse your file. Would you mind filling in some of your history for me?"

"Sure. I've bartended since college. I only started to help pay my way through school, but I soon realized I loved it. After college, I continued to tend bar. My interest was piqued when my boss introduced fancy cocktails to the menu. I trained as a mixologist and here we are."

"What did you study in college?"

"Political Science and it bored me to tears," she laughs, causing those flip flop feelings to ramp up a few notches.

"And you have no regrets? "

"You mean pursuing bar work instead of politics?"

I nod. I want to know what makes her tick. "Yes. Do you wish you had taken a different route?"

"Not at all. Honestly, I only studied Political Science because my parents hounded me to get a degree in something 'solid,' as they put it. But, when I had the space to explore what made me happy, it wasn't politics, it was bartending."

"What is it you love so much?"

"Talking to people, learning about their lives. Don't get me wrong, dealing with drunk assholes is never fun, but nothing in life is perfect. I love the art of mixing a new cocktail, and the creativity it takes to come up with a new recipe."

"Well, you certainly have me sold," I laugh. Erin's passion is intoxicating. Her entire face lights up when she speaks.

"What about you? I mean, I should know more about you considering you're my boss and a Loch." Erin looks a little sheepish. I'm not arrogant enough to think the entire world knows who I am because of my name.

"I'm child number three in the Loch family," I begin. "I have seven siblings. Which is a lot," I laugh. Erin chuckles along, too. "We all have different interests, but I would say we're a close family. My parents worked hard to provide a life that allowed us to pursue our dreams. I always wanted to run bars and clubs."

"Why?"

"I'm not sure, to be honest. Maybe because they offer people some fun and freedom." Erin is studying me. How did my interrogation of her get turned around on me so easily?

"I have to admit that I Googled you," she finally says. "You're quite the entrepreneur in the family. And..."

"And?"

"You have fabulous genetics. I saw a picture of your mother and she doesn't look a day over forty."

Ah yes, another advantage of our genetic coding. Aging slows down to a stop after a vampire mates. Mother and Father are well into their second century of life and yet neither looks older than forty. "Can't complain," I laugh. "I hope I look as good as her when I'm..." I can't finish that sentence because I have honestly forgotten how old mother would be in human years. "Anyway, how are you finding Insomnia? Everything you hoped?"

"Absolutely. I love the clientele and Claire is a fantastic boss."

"About that. I will take over temporarily as the manager."

"Oh, is everything okay?"

"Yes, I just want to give Claire the opportunity to spread her wings. She's overseeing the rest of my venues for a little while."

"Great, well, I look forward to working with you, Amelia."

"Likewise. I see from your schedule that you work a lot of hours." This is where I try to find out subtly if she is seeing anyone. Claire didn't think so, but I need to be sure. "I hope you have a good work-life balance. I can't imagine your partner being happy with the amount of time you spend here." Was that subtle?

"Oh, don't worry, she's fine with it."

Did I hear her correctly? Erin has a girlfriend? Fuck!

# Seven

The universe has to be conspiring against me. Surely you agree. Not only is my mate a human, but she's also a human who has no clue that vampires exist, and has a girlfriend. I might as well let madness take me now.

The conversation with Erin ended pretty quickly after she dropped that bombshell. I hope I didn't appear rude, but my brain kind of shut down. How could Claire not know Erin was seeing someone? Ugh, I can't put this on Claire. I can't even blame Erin; she has no responsibilities towards me.

Erin is busy behind the bar and I'm hiding. My grand plan has been cut off at the knees. What am I supposed to tell my family? Speaking of family, the she-bitch, aka Lucille, is here.

"How goes it, sister?" Lucille asks, sitting next to me. I commandeered a VIP booth for the evening.

"Fantastic," I sigh. My mood is already bad, Lucille's presence is guaranteed to make it worse.

"You're such a shitty liar. What happened? Don't tell me you fucked it up again?"

"Erin has a girlfriend." I have neither the time nor the patience for this conversation.

"And?"

"Of course you wouldn't see a problem with that statement."

"Why would I? Erin is your mate. This other woman is temporary."

"In normal circumstances, I would agree, but this is far from normal. Erin has a choice in this. She isn't driven like me to bond with her other half. There is nothing stopping her from choosing to be with another, or if she so wishes, to be single."

"So that's it? One minor hiccup and you're giving up." Lucille's gaze is all fire and I know she's challenging me.

"I can't force Erin to be mine," I hiss.

"No, but you can fucking fight! You could do so much more than this," she waves her spiny hand at me. "Sitting in the dark feeling sorry for yourself when you haven't even begun. Who is Erin's girlfriend? How long have they been together? Is Erin looking for casual, or more?"

I grit my teeth because admitting Lucille is right makes my blood boil. "I don't know," I state as calmly as possible.

"No, of course you don't, because the moment you stumbled at the first hurdle you gave up. How very disappointing, Amelia."

Enough. "Why are you here?" I growl.

"I'm here to check out Erin."

"Why?"

"Because, despite how much I dislike you ninety percent of the time, you're still my sister."

"Wow, Luce, that was almost nice."

"Almost," she grins, and I can't help but return it. I sigh and tilt my head to the bar.

"That's Erin," I whisper. Lucille is as subtle as a turd in a swimming pool when she cranes her absurdly long neck in Erin's direction.

"Yeah, she's hot."

"She's also human and taken."

Lucille rolls her eyes dramatically. "Excuse me," she calls, and I belatedly realize she's summoning Erin to the booth. *Dear God, what fresh hell is going to unfold now?*

"Amelia, is everything okay?" Erin asks me, smiling sweetly at Lucille.

"Perfect, this is Lucille, one of my sisters."

"Sorry to call you away, Erin. Claire and Amelia have had such wonderful things to say about the latest addition to Insomnia that I couldn't wait to meet you myself." I'll give Lucille one thing. She knows how to dole out the bullshit when needed.

"Wow, that's lovely to hear."

"We're having a family barbecue tomorrow night. Of course you will come, and feel free to bring your other half, if you have one."

Another quality Lucille has is pulling a plan out of her ass last minute. "Yes, you must come along, Erin." Actually, it's the last thing I want to happen. My siblings are trying to push too fast in their excitement. The situation with Erin is delicate and needs a soft touch. Seven members of the Loch family hammering her with questions is not ideal. That's not even including my parents.

"That's a lovely offer, thank you, but I'm working tomorrow evening."

"I'll sort that out," I say.

"Well, okay then. I'm looking forward to it."

"Fabulous. Amelia will give you the address. It's an entirely casual affair. Oh, Amelia, call Claire too."

I nod and give Lucille a tight smile.

"I'd best..." Erin comments, pointing back to the bar.

"Of course. It was a pleasure to meet you."

Lucille and I remain silent for a few moments. I watch Erin's retreating form and Lucille watches me.

"I take it you have a barbecue to arrange now?" I deadpan.

"Indeed. You'll thank me when you're not about to be murdered by one of us in a year's time."

Frankly, that outcome is looking more appealing.

As fast as Lucille swept in, she's flouncing out again. I see Erin track her movements before turning her eyes on me. I give her a small nod and smile, which she returns.

The club is picking up, and the bar is getting busy. I need a distraction, so I decide to help serve customers. It has been a while since I found myself working on this side of a bar, but I love it. My mixing skills are nowhere near Erin's, but I'm not too rusty. I can still make a mean Mojito.

Erin has glanced at me several times since I started serving customers. I guess she is just surprised to see the owner on the front lines. Before I owned my clubs and bars, I started life as a bartender. Of course, I didn't need the money, but I was never good at living off my parents' wealth. In fact, it's not in the Loch DNA to sit on our asses. That's why each of the Loch children are successful in their own right.

Quality investments helped me finance Insomnia. After that, I continued to learn and work hard. Now I spend most of my professional time looking at spreadsheets. It feels good to hold a bottle of liquor in my hands again. Especially when I can still put on a show. Flipping and catching the bottle elicits a cheer and makes me smile. I see Erin raise her eyebrow and grin.

The buzz of the crowd and the music help stave off my personal issues for a little while. I truly can't remember the last time I had this much fun. Erin and I work seamlessly alongside each other. Kit joins us a few hours later. The bar is at full capacity.

By the time I take a break, I'm sweaty and satisfied. Not in the usual way, but I'll take what I can get. Calling Dana is out of the question now. If I had any doubt about Erin being my soulmate, I can put that to rest, because just the thought of touching anyone but her makes my insides coil hideously.

Throughout the evening, I tapped into that feeling I had when we first met. It took me seconds to feel Erin's presence. At one point, I even tested it by sending Erin out into the club to tend to the VIPs. Even with hundreds of bodies occupying the space, I could pick out Erin's movements with pinpoint precision.

Spending time with her in proximity has allowed me to study her better. Although she is small, she is strong. Her biceps and thighs flex when she serves or crouches. Her hair has an array of different shades of blonde in it and her eyes change color with her moods. Erin is fascinating, and my body hums when she is near. It's almost like an electrical current.

My feet ache and all I want to do is slink off to my secret staircase so I can go to bed in the penthouse. But I won't. For once, I'm going to take Lucille's advice. There is still a lot to learn about Erin, and I would harm myself and my family if I simply threw in the towel.

Erin's shift ends, and she heads to the back room. I'm already there with a travel mug of red. I'm parched from all the running around we have done. "Hey, you didn't tell me you were an expert bartender," Erin smiles as she throws on her jacket.

"Not an expert, but I love it."

"I could tell. You looked... at home."

"I started out pulling pints."

"And now you own multiple clubs and bars. Impressive."

"Thank you."

I sip my red and watch her gather her belongings. I wonder where she lives. I could look up her address on her employee record, but that feels like cheating. I also wonder if her girlfriend is waiting for her to return. "Oh, I forgot," I say, grabbing a piece of paper from the table. "Here is my parents' address. Turn up any time around..." Shit, I have no idea when this barbecue is supposed to start. "Actually, I'll have Claire message you with the details. Lucille is likely to change things last minute."

"No problem. Are you sure you want me there?"

"Of course. It's a great way for us to get to know each other."

Those sapphire blues tell me she's feeling curious, and dare I say it, a little attracted to me. I've always been good at reading emotions, especially humans. With Erin, it's curious. I can't tell if the feelings I see in her eyes are hers, or my projection of how I'm feeling. Weird shit happens when vampires mate. Their souls literally blend. I can feel my body and my soul yearning to capture Erin's and intertwine the two together, but there is a blockage. A resistance that seems impenetrable. Is it because Erin simply doesn't see me that way or because I have an issue with her species?

"I look forward to getting to know you better too, Amelia. See you tomorrow."

Everything feels out of focus when Erin is around me now. The world fades and I want to gag at how utterly cliché that sounds. Why didn't my family tell me what finding your mate really feels like? It's confusing, but invigorating. As if my life has taken on a whole new purpose. Shit, what happens to all these feelings if Erin rejects our bond? Will I have to suffer like this until the end?

I shake my head, desperate to rid myself of such melancholic ruminations. It's going to take some time unpacking the thought pattern I have so obviously adopted. The negative reasoning of a vampire who has given up. Now I have felt the presence of my other half, I have to do better. I have a chance.

The penthouse is softly lit. A hot bath soothes my aching form. The echo of my phone irritatingly pulls me from the blissful nothingness I escaped to.

"Yes," I answer, unaware of who is calling.

"Nice way to answer, boss," Claire laughs.

"Sorry, I'm relaxing in a well-earned bath."

"Then I won't take up too much of your time. Lucille called."

"Of course she did."

"Apparently there's a little snafu in your plan to woo Erin."

"She has a girlfriend. Did you know?"

"No, I thought she was single. It must be a relatively new relationship. I wouldn't worry."

"I don't like this," I sigh. "I feel as if I'm manipulating her."

"In what way?"

The thing I love about Claire is her unwavering support and lack of judgment. "I have this information about us. It's life-altering. I'm actively trying to seduce her because my species deems it necessary. But Claire, Erin isn't of our species. It feels wrong, and yet my body is changing. I can feel it already. It's like I've been... activated or something," I chuckle. It's impossible to put what I'm going through in words sufficient to describe it accurately.

"I wish I could give you the answers, Amelia. I think everyone who loves you feels the same. You're in uncharted waters."

"So, what do I do?"

"Forget everyone and everything else. Listen to your body, to your heart. Get to know her, with no expectations or pressure. I think that's the only way you will feel your connection is real."

"Can you tell my family that?" I laugh.

"I can and I will. They're just so excited that you bonded with someone. But, Amelia, if you need them to back off, say it. This is your life. Take control."

"Thank you, Claire, really. I needed to hear that."

"You're welcome. Now, indulge in your bath for a little longer and then get planning. You have a woman to win."

# Eight

The first thing I wanted to do when Erin walked into my parents' backyard was laugh uncontrollably. Seeing her eyes widen so comically at us all was priceless. Can you imagine it? I'm sure Erin felt she'd just walked into a land of giants. Every member of the Loch family is close to or over six feet tall.

Even though she was shocked, Erin didn't shrink back. If anything, she held herself a little higher. I like that in a woman. Erin is no shrinking flower. I saw it the night we met, in her fiery eyes.

The second thing I wanted to do was scoop her into my arms. That's a new feeling to have. I like women; I love sex, and yes, I wanted to find my mate, but I've always been a take it or leave it kind of vampire. There has never been a woman that could invoke such feelings in me. Dana makes me horny, but that's as far as it goes. But here, now looking at Erin, in her tight black jeans and green V-neck t-shirt, I am feeling so much more than lust. She has a softness about her, which contrasts so beautifully with her fierce streak.

Third, I want to groan out loud when a woman walks in behind Erin. I can only presume this is Erin's girlfriend. Whoever the woman is, she doesn't have Erin's grace or ability to conceal her nervousness when confronted with ten tall, raven-haired Lochs.

Claire arrives seconds later, holding two bottles of wine. I am sitting at the back of the yard on the outdoor couch, my arms stretched casually across the back of it. One knee crossed over the other. My goal is to be as cool as possible. Simply because my family is going to be over the top and I need Erin to know that's not who I am. Sure my nerves are fizzing uncomfortably in my stomach, but that's because this barbecue feels like a turning point for how I go forward with Erin.

I have already decided that if Erin seems truly happy with the woman she has brought with her, I will step down. I know it was only last night I was talking about fighting for her, and I haven't reneged on that. However, there is fighting for someone and then there is controlling them. Erin is a free spirited, strong woman. Who the hell am I to interfere? That's why I will do nothing but be myself and hope she chooses me.

My family doesn't know my intentions, and that's how it will stay. None of my siblings or parents can see things clearly, not when my life is on the chopping block. They will do everything they can to make Erin mine. But that's not what I want.

I want Erin to choose me and love me because we are meant to be together. That takes time and trust. We need to build a friendship and a sound foundation. That won't happen if our relationship is built on manipulation and lies.

How I tell her we are vampires is still unknown. I mean, how the hell does a conversation like that go? What I *have* decided is that I will befriend her and then tell her before I make any romantic overtures. Depending on whether the woman she is with is still in the picture.

My mother is the first one to greet Erin, followed by my father, Laurence and then Marcus. Lucille hangs in the shadows, watching, which comes as little surprise. My sister will watch and size up the situation before making her move.

Aliah, Jacob, and Maria are standing by the grill chatting to each other, happy to wait their turn. Claire spots me and winks. Sipping on my martini, I calculate the best time to introduce myself. I said I wouldn't manipulate her, but that doesn't mean I won't give it my best shot to be alluring.

The clothes I'm wearing highlight my best assets. Pinstripe slacks caress my ass, making it pop. The silk tank top rides low enough that my cleavage is just the right amount of sexy without being too obvious. As usual, my black hair hangs straight down my back. I've perfected my eye make-up, and the plum lipstick works well, too.

Once my parents have finished their initial interrogation, I see my opportunity. Erin looks over at me and that's when I make my move. Without breaking eye contact, I uncross my legs and stand gracefully. The added sway in my hips is a success. Erin's eyes dip to watch me walk. My heart is thudding from the heat I feel smoldering in my chest. Erin's pupils are so large her eyes are almost black, and I know right then she wants me.

"Erin, welcome," I purr, leaning down, brushing my lips against her cheek. Am I playing dirty? Maybe. "And this must be?"

"Mack," she sputters. "Mackenzie North."

"It's a pleasure." It's not, but I can't exactly say that. Now I've seen the woman up close, I recognize her. She frequents Insomnia.

"Thank you for inviting us," Mack smiles, but it's tight. "You have a lovely home."

"Not mine, I'm afraid. My parents', and, yes, they love it."

"Oh, so you don't live here then?"

"God no. Just here for a visit."

"It was Amelia's birthday last week. We had some partying to do," Lucille adds, gliding up beside me. Mack tries to give Lucille's body a subtle scan. Both Lucille and I notice and then I understand Lucille's timing. She's testing and clearly whatever her assumption was, she's smug about being correct. "I'm Lucille Loch." She offers Mack her hand, which is taken immediately.

"Shall we get a drink?" I offer to everyone. Lucille's games don't surprise me, but that doesn't mean I'm comfortable. "Erin, why don't you and Mack take a seat. We'll grab something for us all."

"Okay, thank you." Erin has a small tinge of red on her cheeks that is adorable.

Making my way over to the bar, I pull Lucille close. "No games, Luce. Understand? I don't want you interfering with them."

Lucille tuts and rolls her eyes. "Come on, Amelia."

"No." I state. Leaving no room for argument. She huffs but doesn't protest further. We collect a tray of champagne and head over to the seating area.

"What is it you do, Mack?" I ask, handing out flutes of champagne. More of my family have gravitated over.

"I'm a pediatrician," she answers. Wonderful, she helps sick kids. I make money off of drunk people. Score one for Mack.

"Admirable. Thank you for everything you do," I say, meaning every word. "It must be hard sometimes."

"Oh, for sure, but it's my passion. I have wanted to be a doctor since I was small. The hours are long, but the kids are worth every sleep-deprived second," Mack laughs. Dammit, she's a nice person too.

"At least she gets my strange hours," Erin adds with a smile.

"Please let me know if you need to change your hours, Erin," I say. "We want you to be happy at Insomnia."

"I am," she rushes to say. "I have zero complaints. I've always been an owl, staying awake until the early hours."

"If you're sure."

"Positive. Really!" Our eyes stay locked, and I know I need to tread lightly. My body is betraying me. The pull of her is magnetic and rather distracting. Thankfully, my parents' timing is right on point. They join us right on time to save me from doing anything stupid.

The conversation shifts, allowing me to take a breath. That's the good thing about a large family. No one stays the center of attention for long. Jacob regales us with stories from his office. Mack still looks a little out of place. I think the sheer number of us is overwhelming for her.

Mack stands a little taller than Erin, but not by much. Compared to the Lochs she is small. Her hair is chestnut and hangs just below her shoulders. I can't say she's not pretty. I wish I could. It's understandable why Erin is attracted to her.

Erin is happily talking to my family. She's not shy. Claire is sitting on Maria's knee again. We have enough chairs, but that seems to be their thing, I suppose. I tune back into the conversation in time to hear Erin laughing with my siblings. "... You're all freakishly tall. Has anyone ever told you that?" she chuckles.

Every single Loch is enamored with her. This is both wonderful and awful. There is no way they are going to allow me to do this my own way. "Or you are just very short," Aliah laughs.

"It's true," Erin sighs playfully. "Both my parents are small. It's not fair."

"Oh, I don't know. What's that saying? Ah yes... all good things come in small packages," my father smiles.

"I like you, Mr. Loch," Erin laughs, pointing at him.

"Harlan, please. No need to be so formal."

"And you must call me Victoria. I insist."

I see Mack discreetly pull her phone out and sigh. She leans in and whispers something into Erin's ear. "I'm so sorry, but I have to go. A patient needs me."

"Of course. I hope everything is okay." I admire Mack. Erin has clearly found a good one.

"I'll call you," Mack says softly to Erin before giving her a quick kiss on the cheek.

"Well, that sucks," Jacob sighs a little too dramatically. No one apart from Erin is sorry that Mack has left.

"Let's eat," my mother calls.

While the brood organize themselves, I hang back with Erin. Getting ten people to sit at a dining table is a tall order in this family. Bickering is a certainty, and I'd rather not get involved. Erin is standing back, chuckling at my family. I'm standing back, looking at her.

"Sorry Mack had to go."

"It's fine. It's not the first and won't be the last time she has to leave."

"She seems lovely."

"It's still new, but I like her."

My gut twists. I'm in purgatory. Is that my cue to stop, to leave Erin to her own fate? "I'm sure the feeling is mutual."

"What about you? Anyone in your life?" Erin asks easily.

"It's complicated," I say because let's face it, this whole thing is a cluster fuck.

Erin scratches the back of her neck. Her body language is reading; uncomfortable. "Are you with that woman?"

"Which woman?"

"Um, the one you took upstairs on your birthday."

"Dana? No, she's married."

"Married, but you—"

"She's poly. But I'm not interested in a relationship with her."

"Just a good time in the sack, huh?" I smirk and look at Erin, who has gone beet red. "I'm so sorry. That was rude.

Jesus, I don't know why I keep blurting shit out around you."

My shoulders shake with laughter. "It's fine. You're quite entertaining when you *blurt shit out*." I wink for effect, and it works. "Me and Dana are just a bit of fun. She's not my soulmate."

"You believe in soulmates?" Erin's voice is softer, and she's turned her body towards me. I mirror her stance.

"I do. I believe there is a person for everyone. The other half of a soul destined to love you."

"I think a love like that would scare me," Erin confesses, her voice even quieter. Our bodies have moved a fraction closer. Is she feeling the pull, too?

"A love like that would be worth the fear," I whisper.

"Burgers are up," my father shouts, causing us both to jump. I clear my throat and hope I can inhale enough oxygen to stop me from passing out.

"Let's eat," I say, smiling. Erin is looking at me with confusion. I think she is struggling to understand what is happening between us.

"Oh, Erin, do you like boats?" My mother asks.

"I love boats," she smiles.

"We're going out this weekend. Will you join us?"

"Oh, that's kind of you, but I'm working."

"Kit is working this weekend," I say. "She asked to swap shifts. I'm sorry I forgot to tell you."

"Oh, no problem, um, I'll need to ask Mack if she has anything planned for us."

"Bring her along," Lucille calls from the far end of the table.

This is not at all going according to plan.

# Nine

Guilt is a strange feeling. It serves no purpose, really. Once something is done, it can't be undone. And yet, I feel guilty because I am pursuing Erin, even though she is taken. Mack is a good person, and all who attended the barbecue could see she is enamored with Erin.

But when I looked into Erin's eyes, I could see she wanted more. You might call bullshit on that. Say I'm seeing what I want to see, and you could be correct in that assumption. Erin does like Mack, but there is no passion. I'll keep to my word and play fair, but I am going after what I want.

Today is going to be a juggling act. I desperately want to flirt with Erin, but Mack will be with her. I won't disrespect the doctor outright. Instead, I will put on my smallest bikini and hope for a reaction.

Boat days are usually fun. The family heads out on the water as often as possible. Mother and Father have hosted hundreds of guests on the family yacht. Today will be a low-key affair but equally important as one of their soirees.

After Erin had left the barbecue, I gathered the family and gave them a lecture. No more interfering. They agreed a little too quickly, but I'll take what I can get for now. The harbor is not far, but I need a little time to collect myself. Throwing my leathers on, I hop on my bike. A pleasant cruise along the coastline is in order.

Everyone is waiting for me, including Erin and Mack. Time slipped away from me as it usually does when I'm on a motorcycle. Although, this is perfect because Erin is staring at me as I glide to a stop in front of them all. Tugging my helmet off, I shake out my long hair. Erin's eyes grow wide, and I smile. Next is my leathers. It's not difficult to make bike leathers sexy.

"Sorry I'm late," I say.

"I didn't know you rode a motorcycle," Erin blurts. I see the amusement in everyone's eyes, except Mack's.

"I've ridden for years," I answer.

"She gets it from me," Mom calls over.

"Do you like bikes?" I ask Erin.

"I've never been on one. But I have always wanted to try."

"I'd be happy to give you a ride. You too, Mack, if you're interested?"

"No thank you," Mack answers curtly. "Motorcycles are extremely dangerous."

"Indeed, as are many things in this life," I reply kindly.

My parents break the sudden tension by ushering us all down the gangway to the boat. There is a beautiful spread of food and wine waiting for us. My family shows love through feeding.

Once everyone has eaten their fill, we splinter off into groups. Lucas, Maria and Jacob head for the pool. Lucille, Aliah and Laurence make themselves at home at the bar. Mother, Father, Erin, Mack and I settle on the loungers. Cocktails in hand, we converse politely. The boat slowly makes its way out to sea.

Ever since Erin checked me out at the harbor, Mack's attitude towards me has cooled considerably. The small talk is getting on my nerves, especially because I cannot say a single word to Erin without Mack answering for her.

Putting my empty cocktail glass down, I stand and strip off my light linen trousers and top to reveal the bikini I took extra care picking. Bingo! Erin blushes, her eyes do a quick sweep of my body. Pretending I haven't noticed her wandering eye, I head to the pool. A little extra swing in my hips.

The water is delicious on my overheated skin. Lucas and Jacob are at one end of the pool fighting playfully. Maria swims over to me. "You caught the look, right?" she whispers.

"Which one?" I chuckle.

"You're devious, Amelia," Maria grins.

"I'm simply cooling off."

"And the bike leathers?"

"I needed a ride to clear my head. Leathers are a must, you know that."

"Uh huh," she laughs.

"Mind if we join you?" Erin asks from behind me. I turn and have to stifle my surprise. Erin is in a forest green two-piece. Her hair is swept up in a messy bun. My God, her body is magnificent. Curves for days. A swift kick from Maria brings me back down to earth. Mack is standing beside her, frowning at my obvious ogling. I can't help it, really I can't.

"Sure, jump in," Maria says, covering for my lack of sound or movement. Erin slides into the pool and I have to take a step back. Something is happening inside of my body. I must actively fight with myself not to take her in my arms and devour her. Is this how every vampire feels when they can't be with their mate? If so, it is awful. I wouldn't wish this on my worst enemy. I wouldn't even wish it on Lucille.

"I love your swimsuit," Maria babbles.

"Oh, thanks. I picked it up last month."

"And yours too, Mack." Maria adds belatedly.

"Thanks."

My ears are buzzing, and my stomach is cramping. This can't be right. Turning to the pool wall, I haul myself out of the water and frantically scour the deck for my mother. She's inside, talking to a member of the crew. Racing in, I forgo a towel. Who gives a shit about water pooling inside when my body feels like it's going to explode?

"Mom," I say with as much urgency as I can muster. She takes one look at me and scoops me by the arm towards the master bedroom.

"Amelia, what's wrong?"

"Something... isn't... right," I gasp. The tightness in my stomach is getting worse. My hands claw at my skin.

"Harlan!" she screams through the door. Only seconds pass before my father enters the room. His eyes grow wide when he sees me doubled over.

"Get a bottle of red now." My father doesn't question my mother's order. He rushes out the door. "Tell me what's happening," Mom asks calmly.

I try to describe the pain in my stomach and when it began to hurt. Dad barges in, thrusting a matte black bottle at my mom. "Drink this, honey." The blood soothes my stomach momentarily, but the ache is returning.

"What's wrong with me?"

My parents share a worried look. "We need to get you to a doctor." That's all my father says before leaving again. The boat makes an audible groan as the captain changes course. We are heading back to land. Thoughts of Erin flicker across my eyelids. The sudden increase in pain makes me scream out loud. I feel my mother's hand trying to soothe me. The gentle caress across my forehead does nothing to rid me of this pain.

What feels like hours pass. Lucas and Marcus lift me from the bed. We must be back at the harbor. "It's okay, Amelia," Lucas whispers in my ear. Nothing feels okay. We pass my family and then I see Erin. Her face is pale, and I wish I could comfort her, but then I see Mack put her hand on Erin's waist and the fire that burns in my abdomen becomes too much to handle. Everything turns black.

The smell of lavender infiltrates my senses. Crinkling my nose, I try to pull myself away from the disgusting scent. "Wake up, Amelia," a voice I don't recognize says. Light seeps through my eyelids. Opening them, I wince at the throbbing in my head. My stomach aches horrendously.

"What..."

"It's okay, baby," my mother coos.

I take a few minutes to fully come around. I'm in my bedroom at my parents' house. "What happened?"

"Sit up and we'll try to explain." Lucille says. Her tone is far too kind. Maybe I should be worried.

Sitting up, I take a sip of red. My entire family is in the room looking at me. It's unnerving. "Tell me," I croak. My mind is already forming conclusions that scare the shit out of me.

"This is Doctor Mendhi," my father says, gesturing to a kind-looking gentleman who is smiling at me.

"Hello," I say stupidly.

"Good afternoon, Amelia. How are you feeling now?"

"My stomach still hurts, and I have a headache."

"To be expected."

"Am I turning?" I blurt out because that is the singular worry whizzing around my mind.

"No Amelia, you're not. You are experiencing some side effects, though."

"Side effects of what?"

"Your bond to Erin," mother explains. None of this is making sense.

"I don't understand." I want to scream at them to hurry the hell up and explain what is going on.

"Oh, for fuck sakes," Lucille sighs. "Stop pussyfooting around her. Amelia, the fact that you have found your mate but haven't bonded is causing physical side effects. The closer you get to Erin, without sealing your souls, the worse you're going to feel."

"Honey, you need to talk to Erin." Mother talks softly to me like I'm a child.

"It's not that simple and you know it," I grind out.

"This is a unique case," Dr. Mendhi interjects before my mom can reply to me. "I can't tell you if the side effects will get worse for certain. It's an educated guess. I would like to monitor you over the next few weeks. Or until you can cement your bond."

"Have you ever dealt with this before?" I ask.

"Once," he states and grows quiet. I definitely do not want to know what happened to the vampire in question. "I suggest you get some rest now. Stay hydrated, and call if you need me."

As soon as the good doctor is gone, my mother swoops down on me like a vulture, ready to pick at me until I surrender. Holding my hand up to stop her, I take a moment. "I know what you're going to say. Please don't. I meant what I said. I'm doing this my way. Of course, I will take into consideration the physical side effects I'm going to suffer. But please, I beg you all to let me handle this."

"Okay, love—"

"Harlan," Mother barks.

"Victoria, Amelia is right. This has to be her way. We would never dream of interfering with another vampire's mating. We cannot do that now."

"But this isn't a normal mating," Mother spits.

"No, it's not. We don't know how it will work out, but we have to trust our daughter to do what is best for her and Erin."

"Please, Mom, don't fight me on this."

"Ridiculous!" she snaps, storming out of the room.

"Can I have a minute with Amelia?" Marcus asks. My family filters out after giving me kisses. Lucille socks me in the arm instead. That makes me feel better.

"Are you going to argue, Marcus?"

"No, I understand, and I agree with you. However, you have to adapt to this new information. I'm not sure you can take things as slow as you would like with Erin, not now."

Begrudgingly, I know he is right. If the pain I felt today is just the beginning of the side effects, I hate to think about what is to come. "I need to think."

"Yes, you do." He leans in and kisses me on my head.

Finally, I am alone. Without delay, Erin's face swims through my mind. The ache in my stomach pulses. How am I going to get through this in one piece? Marcus is right. I need to adapt my approach. As much as I would love to get to know Erin over the next several months before making my interest known, I can't wait that long.

Chuckling, I think how ridiculous I sound. Erin surely knows where my interest lies. What she doesn't know is how my very soul aches for her. That her presence is causing me pain. That she is the one person on this entire planet that can make me whole.

# Ten

My mother has me mainlining red, like that's going to solve all my issues. Her constant scowl is the residue of yesterday's discussion. She is furious that I will not let her, or my family involve themselves. I have tried to reason with her over the past twenty-four hours, but it is in vain. Victoria Loch is the most stubborn and hardheaded vampire I have ever known.

"Mother, if I drink anymore, I'm going to pee the bed. Please don't make me suffer that indignity." My playful tone finally elicits a nano grin.

"Fine. I'll leave it on your bedside table."

"Thank you."

She spends the next few minutes tidying my already immaculate room. I understand she is worried, but she's driving me to distraction.

Marcus knocks on the already open door. He has taken to popping into my room about as frequently as Mother. I never pegged him as a mother hen type. "Amelia, you have a guest. Are you feeling up to a visit?"

"Yes, who is it?"

"Erin."

Just the sound of her name jolts my heart. I snap my focus to my mother. She shakes her head at me. "I didn't invite her." Her answer satisfies me. Mother might be bull-headed, but she would never go against my wishes.

"Of course, send her in." Suddenly I feel self-conscious. Being laid up in bed all day can't be a good look on me. I haven't even brushed my hair.

"H-hi," Erin says quietly, her eyes wide. Erin is a woman who wears her emotions on her face. Right now, she looks as scared as she did yesterday on the boat when my brothers carried me off in their arms.

"Erin, hello, come," I say as animatedly as possible. Gesturing her to sit on the bed. The ache in my stomach is intensifying with every step she takes towards me.

"How... how are you?"

"Just fine. Turns out I have a stomach ulcer."

"Oh, no." Her hand reflexively jolts to my forearm. The brush of her fingertips on my skin cools the burning in my abdomen. That's interesting.

"I'll be just fine." I smile, setting my other hand over hers. A pulse echoes through my body. It isn't pleasurable, more like a calming ripple. The ache in my stomach disappears entirely.

"When I saw you being carried by your brothers with blood coming from your mouth—" Erin is unable to finish her sentence. A small sob escapes her throat. I must have spilled red down myself on the boat. And poor Erin believes it was my blood.

Leaning towards her, I take my hand from hers and cup her face. "Erin, I'm okay, I promise." It's a false promise, because I am far from okay, but I cannot stand to see the anguish on her beautiful face a moment longer.

The pulsing picks up speed and is now filling my chest. My body once again feels pulled to her. Erin is leaning into my hand. She must be feeling it, too. Our faces are inches apart, but in a second, Erin pulls herself away. The look of realization on her face stings me. "I-I have to go. I'm working tonight," she stutters, clearly flustered. Probably very confused as to why she nearly kissed me. As far as I know, she is still with Mack. But, like me, I'm guessing her body is reacting to our connection.

"I'll see you soon," I reply calmly. "I will be setting up residence permanently in the penthouse." I hadn't decided that until this very second. If I'm to stand any chance of winning Erin's heart, I need to be close to her.

"Right, okay. Great, okay... yes, so I'll see you soon then." Her rambling is delightful, and her pink-tinged cheeks are delectable.

"You will." The smoothness of my voice melts her. I can see it. Something else to store away for later use.

The moment Erin is gone, I call for my mother, who unbeknownst to me had left the room. I swear, when Erin is present, my world is only big enough to see her. "Mother, call the doctor."

She rushes to my side in a panic. "What happened?"

"I'm not sure, but I need to tell him. I think it's important." Like a flash of lightning, she is there one second and gone the next. I wonder if my parents have the doctor stowed somewhere in the house because he arrives mere minutes later.

"Victoria informs me you have something to tell me."

"Erin was here. I felt the same pain when she entered the room, but then, when she touched my skin, the ache abated. I lay my hand on hers and the discomfort evaporated entirely."

"Interesting." I allow him a few minutes of silent contemplation. As much as I want to bark at him for an answer, there is no point. "I need you to tell me the exact context of the touch."

Sparing no detail, I recount Erin's visit. "What does it mean?"

"From what you have told me, Erin was experiencing a strong emotional reaction. When she touched you, it was out of concern. My best guess, and I am sorry, but *it is* only a guess, is that the concern she showed you was genuine emotion. Erin cares for you and that simple act of touching you was a balm to the side effects you were suffering."

The doctor's educated guess should provide me with relief, but it doesn't. It just reminds me, once again, that I need Erin's love to cure my malady. I can't expect her to touch me like that every time I see her.

"What happens if I stay away from her? Keep my distance."

"You will expedite your symptoms; of that, I am sure."

"But if she isn't near me, I can't feel the pull, therefore no symptoms."

"It doesn't work like that, Amelia. Your body—your soul—will only cope for so long being away from Erin. No distance will sever the bond you have to her."

"So I have only pain and suffering to look forward to. Fantastic. You can leave now."

Bowing his head, Dr. Mendhi retreats. I'm royally fucked either way. If I get near her, I'm in pain constantly, but if I stay away, I will probably die quicker, or worse, suffer madness.

The room feels claustrophobic. I cannot sit in this bed a second longer. Ripping back the covers, I stumble my way to the shower. The water does nothing to soothe me, but at least I won't stink. Hurrah for small wins.

Considering my mother or Marcus haven't immediately come back to my room means they are peppering the good doctor with questions. That's fine. It allows me some precious minutes alone.

Feeling out of control enrages me. For the sake of my family and our relationship, I need to leave the house. They will all cry bloody murder, but it's tough. There is no point in sitting around, as they all fuss over me.

"And where the hell do you think you're going?" Mother screeches. Ah, and the peace is shattered.

"I'm going to the club. I need to arrange for my possessions to be shipped to the penthouse."

"Amelia, you need to rest."

"No, I don't. What I need is some time to figure this nightmare out. And, as I'm sure you are now aware, I need to be closer to Erin, so I don't give myself a heart attack or whatever."

"Can you not speak like that?" she pleads.

"I'm sorry, truly. I know you're scared, Mother, but I have to go."

"Let one of your siblings accompany you. At least do that for me."

"Fine." If I don't concede, she will be in the penthouse, hounding me. I know her too well. "Tell Lucille to pack a bag."

Her eyes widen. "Lucille?" I have to chuckle. Out of all of my siblings, Lucille would usually be the last one I would voluntarily choose to have in my house. But, in this circumstance, she is the one I need.

"Yes. Lucille." Turning my back, I end the conversation. I know I must come across as rude, but trust me. Sometimes it is the only way to get my mother to back off.

Hearing the door close, I know she has gone to find Lucille. A small grin blossoms on my face out of sheer devilment. Lucille is going to be pissed, and that makes me feel a little better.

Stomping in the hallway notifies me of Lucille's impending arrival. "Why do this, Amelia? Why torture us both?"

"Why not? If I'm going to be miserable, you might as well come along for the ride."

"You're such a... ugh, I can't even stay mad. Well played, sister, well played. I would have absolutely done the same thing."

"I'm glad you approve," I chuckle.

"Seriously though, wouldn't you prefer Laurence or Marcus to live with you?"

"Will you coddle me? Treat me like I'm a child?"

"You already know the answer to that."

"Therefore, you already know the answer to why I want you at the penthouse with me rather than any of our siblings. My tolerance is already at full capacity."

"Fair. Know that I won't suffer wallowing, Amelia. Not like your birthday."

"That was you suffering? Lucille, you ripped the covers off me."

"But I didn't drag you out of bed, did I?"

"True."

"So, care to tell me what the doctor was summoned for?"

I fill her in on the details. There is no point keeping anything from my family. "I figured it's better for me to stay close to Erin. At least the club offers me that excuse. Gives me time to plan my next move."

"Your next move is to ask her out."

"While she still has a girlfriend?"

"Sure it's tacky, but, hey, clearly Erin has feelings for you. I would bet she doesn't understand them. If you push too hard, I think she'll retreat. But, you have to do something, Amelia."

"I know," I sigh. "Let me have a couple of days to gather my thoughts. I can't do this half-cocked."

"Agreed. We can use the time to watch her a little closer."

"That is creepy as hell, Lucille."

"And yet we still have to do it. Do you think you're going to be alright, being so close to her but—"

"Not being able to touch her?" Lucille nods at me. "I have no choice, sister."

After a few more protests from my mother, I finally escape to Insomnia. The club is dark for another few hours. Erin will be inside though, setting up. I want to go to her immediately, but I don't. Instead, I slip in undetected with

Lucille and head to my apartment. We unpack what we have and then set about organizing my belongings to be shipped. I have no idea how long I will have to stay here.

"Get dressed. We're going downstairs," Lucille instructs from the doorway to my bedroom.

"I'm beat." My words fall on deaf ears. Lucille strides in and goes straight to my closet, picking out my blood-red corset and black fitted pants.

"Get dressed," she demands. We stay frozen, staring at each other in a silent battle of wills. I clamp my jaw, knowing I'm about to concede defeat.

"Fine."

"You have ten minutes."

Already I regret my choice of housemate. Still, I get myself ready with a couple of minutes to spare. The three-inch heels I choose make me feel strong. I'm going to tower over most people, and that's what I need. Some form of control and power.

We descend the private stairs and enter the club. The crowd is vast, and the air is electric. I scan the area, happy there are no problems. The bar is busy, so I leave Lucille by herself to help out. Of course Erin is serving. I try my best to act like there is no big deal. Slipping behind the bar, I take orders.

The ache in my stomach is there, but I know the moment Erin spots me because the ache turns into a ripple once again. That means she is looking at me. That means she is feeling strong, caring emotions. That means there is hope!

# Eleven

"Are you ready?" Lucille asks for the tenth time. My answer is a resounding no. For over a week I have been working closely with Erin. Always the professional as my insides sear in pain. But I know I have to take my time. Making sure Erin is comfortable around me is essential.

We've shared some laughs and worked several packed evenings behind the bar together, which was an outstanding success. Insomnia is my flagship club, and it shows. It's the hottest place in Los Angeles.

Lucille has been abnormally patient with me. I expected her to bulldoze her way into my affairs, but I have been proven wrong. She's even fielded calls and visits from my mother and Marcus.

That is, until this evening. Sitting with a glass of wine on the balcony, I'm surprised by Lucille's presence. She is supposed to be visiting her husband and son. Yet, she isn't. She's here, scowling at me.

"I'm not ready. It's too soon." Approaching Erin and asking her out formally is eating away at my conscience. She is still with Mack, and they seem to be doing well.

"Tough, times up," Lucille growls. "I know you are in constant pain, Amelia; you don't think I see your face twitch in agony?"

"I'm fine." I'm not. As the days pass by, the pain in my abdomen is getting worse.

"No, you're not. It's time to make a move."

"Not yet," I hiss.

"Okay." Turning, Lucille leaves me. I am completely perplexed. Lucille never agrees so easily. *Idiot!*

Slamming down my wine, I chase after Lucille. As I thought, she's heading downstairs. Barging through the door, I see her approach Erin. "God damn it, Lucille," I growl, marching over to them.

Slowing my pace, I try to calm my murderous feelings towards my sister. "So Erin," I hear Lucille say. "Are you and Mack exclusive?"

"Oh, um—"

"You do not have to answer that, Erin. Please excuse my sister."

"I'm only asking," Lucille sighs.

"It's okay, um, we've been seeing each other for a few weeks. But we haven't had the conversation about exclusivity yet."

"So, does that mean you would be interested in dating other people?"

Erin's cheeks blush. She looks between me and Lucille. "Um, that's really flattering Lucille, but—"

"Not me!" Lucille barks out, laughing.

"Oh?" Erin answers scrunching up her face.

I am begging Lucille to shut her fucking mouth, but it's too late. "I meant Amelia."

The air is ripped from my lungs. The murderous rage I successfully calmed only seconds ago is surging through every molecule of my body. Frozen in place, I stare blankly at Lucille. I cannot believe she did that.

Erin's throat clearing startles me. I've yet to look at her, afraid of what I will see.

"Anyway, just thought I'd ask. See you later, sis."

My eyes track the traitorous hag all the way out of the club. Running away would be wrong, but I'm seriously considering it. That is until I feel warmth spread from my hand. I close my eyes briefly to bask in Erin's touch. Shifting my focus back to the room, I turn and finally meet her eyes.

"Why did Lucille ask that?" Erin's eyes are as soft as her voice. I swallow several times before answering.

"Because I wanted to ask you out, but I didn't know where things were with you and Mack, and I would never want to put you in an uncomfortable position." As I'm answering Erin, I am plotting Lucille's demise. "I'm truly sorry if Lucille has made you feel that way. I'll talk to her."

"It's okay," she answers quickly. My heart feels like it's everywhere but where it should be. I can feel the pulse in my feet, neck, and wrists. Oh God, am I actually having a heart attack? I know I made an offhand comment to my mother, but I didn't really think Erin could cause my heart to explode.

"I..."

"Do you... um, do you still want to ask me out?"

The smooth version of myself is nowhere to be seen. I'm a mess. All I can do is move my head. Am I nodding? I hope so. A small smile graces Erin's face. She dips her head to hide her smirk. A few seconds pass before she lifts herself up, looking me in the eye with a playful glint.

"You haven't asked me anything yet."

"Oh, um, right... Erin... will you... I mean, would you like to go on a date with me?"

"Okay." One word is all it takes for me to feel like fireworks are whizzing around my chest.

"Are you free tomorrow?" My confidence is returning. Erin didn't reject me. I didn't realize how much the thought of that happening was weighing on me.

"I'm out with Mack tomorrow," Erin begins. I ignore the stab in my gut. "I think it's only fair that I let her know I'm planning on dating you."

"Of course. Whatever you want."

"What about Saturday? I have it off. My boss is good like that," she smiles.

"Yes!" I blurt. I have zero game with Erin.

"That's settled then. Should we meet here?"

"Yes, shall we say eight?" I'm already planning the perfect night.

"Great. Well, I should get the bar ready. We open soon." We both linger a few more seconds.

"I'll see you later," I say eventually. I'd love nothing more than to stand there all night looking at Erin, but first I need to find Lucille.

Walking backwards, I give Erin my best smile before turning around and heading back up to the penthouse. Like the flip of a switch, I go from joyfully happy to searing mad.

Lucille is lounging on the sofa when I storm in. She looks as if she has no care in the world. I'm about to slap some into her. "What the fuck was that?" I scream. It's not like me to lose all control, but with Lucille, it happens. "I asked you to let me do this my way, but oh no, you're just like every fucker else who thinks they know better. This is my life, Lucille. Mine!" I roar. Lucille hasn't batted an eye which makes me rage more.

"Did she say yes?" she simply asks, and all my righteous anger evaporates in a puff. God damn Lucille.

Saturday has taken a millennium to arrive. Lucille has spent the last several days gloating obnoxiously. I told her to pack her bags and go, but she refused. We spent an hour glaring at each other before I gave up and sulked in my room. How is she the younger sibling?

Time away from Erin is becoming more difficult. I didn't realize until I hadn't been close to her for forty-eight hours. Not only were the cramps excruciating, but I suffered nosebleeds, too. Lucille wanted to call Dr. Mendhi, but what's the point? He's only going to tell me what I already know. At least I've made progress with Erin, though. Yes, Lucille was the reason for that, but that doesn't mean I can't stay pissed at her for as long as possible.

Taking a few calming breaths, I head downstairs. Erin should be here in a few minutes. Maybe a shot of vodka will help settle my nerves. A shot of vodka won't be enough. Not for the vision standing in front of me as I enter the bar. Erin looks divine. She is wearing a green summer dress that tapers in at the waist. Her hair is braided to one side. She looks like a goddamn goddess.

My nerves are shot. I can feel my hands shaking. It's like my soul is excited and channeling that energy into my extremities. *Calm down, just relax.*

"Erin, you look superb." I love giving a woman a compliment. Erin deserves all the compliments.

"Why, Ms. Loch, that's very kind of you to say."

I like the playful side of her. "Are you ready?" I ask.

"Lead the way."

My palms are a little sweaty as I head towards the staircase. Unlike other dates I've taken out, I don't plan to wine and dine Erin in a flashy restaurant. Not that she doesn't deserve it. I just want us to be alone and relaxed. Cooking for Erin is intimate, and I hope she isn't disappointed.

"Is this okay?" I ask when we step through my apartment door. There is a candlelit table on the balcony. The lights are dimmed, and the music is soft.

"It's wonderful," she responds.

"Do you like tagine?" Moroccan food is one of my favorite things to cook.

"I love it. It's been ages since I've had the chance to eat any, though."

"Would you like some wine? Or beer? I have everything."

"Wine is great. I didn't tell you how lovely you look tonight." Erin is standing close to me, her eyes giving me an appreciative once over.

"Thank you." I tried to go smart casual. Jeans and a strappy top. For once, I have my hair up in a low bun.

Erin's phone interrupts the mutual appreciation. Leaving her to answer whoever is texting her, I check on the food. "Sorry about that. It was Mack confirming our plans for Tuesday."

The stabbing pain in my gut is worse this time 'round. I know I can't rush things with Erin, and I have no right to ask her to stop seeing Mack, but my soul doesn't understand that. So for now, I need to suck it up and deal.

"Going anywhere nice?" I ask. This is a weird conversation to be having on a first date, right?

"Amelia, I'm not here to talk about me and Mack."

"Sorry, of course. Why don't you sit at the table, and I'll dish up."

Everything seems so tense between us. Where is that easy vibe we had? Is it me? Am I giving off weird energy or something? Maybe I'm overthinking things. "Amelia?" I didn't realize Erin was still standing near me. "You seem to be nervous."

"I suppose I am a little."

"Why? It's just me. Would it make you feel better if I started yelling at you again?"

A short burst of laughter escapes my throat. "Maybe," I jest.

"Come on. Let's sit down with this delicious smelling meal you cooked for me and just talk. No pressure."

Smiling warmly at Erin, I gently take her hand and kiss her knuckles in gratitude. With just a few words, she has relaxed me. "Sit, I'll bring everything over."

My lips are tingling from the touch of Erin's skin. Her eyes are pools of blue and once again I am mesmerized by her. Turning to the kitchen, I smile when I hear her let out a ragged breath. She must be feeling this. Surely!

The rest of the evening goes by with an ease I've never felt before. Talking to Erin is as easy as breathing. She comments on the view; I comment again on how gorgeous she looks. We chat about previous jobs, college, girlfriends. Everything but the one thing I so desperately want to talk about. The fact she is sitting with a vampire.

I promised myself that I would tell Erin everything before making any kind of romantic move. So far, my plans are not going the way I expected. Now I have to admit, I'm terrified at the prospect of telling her. She's going to think I'm insane if I start harping on about vampires and soulmates.

"You've disappeared on me again." Erin's hand has made its way over the table and it's resting on my balled fist.

"Sorry, no, I'm here." This whole zoning out thing needs to stop. I can't keep getting in my head, not when she's here.

"Are you sure? Do you need me to go?"

A pain sears through my chest. I grit my teeth, placing my free hand over Erin's. Screwing my eyes shut, I stroke her hand gently, hoping the pain will pass soon. Suddenly, all contact is lost. I can't even open my eyes to see if she's leaving. Then I feel her by my side. She's crouching down next to me. Her hands reach up and cup my face so very tenderly. Like the sun breaking through stormy skies, my mind clears, my body relaxes, and the pain fades.

If Erin decides I am not the one for her, falling into madness will be the least of my worries. I know now I cannot live without this woman.

# Twelve

As far as Erin is concerned, I took a bit of a turn last night. She still thinks my problem is a stomach ulcer. As you can imagine, it utterly ruined the mood. I sent Erin home with a quick peck on the cheek and a promise to see my doctor.

My mood has never been lower than it is right now. I feel like I can't do right for doing wrong. I get close to her, and it hurts, which in turn hurts her, or at least scares her. The look on her face as she tried to soothe me last night was unforgettable, and not in a good way.

Barging through my parents' front door, I bark for the doctor. I know he's still here. There is a flurry of movement, and sure enough, my family comes running. The urge to roll my eyes at them all is overwhelming. Why are my siblings still here? They all have lives to lead. Their presence isn't solving anything.

"Amelia, what's wrong?" My mother asks in her usual panicked state.

"Where is Dr. Mendhi?" There will be time for conversation later.

A door opens behind me and the doctor hurries over. "Amelia?"

"This isn't good enough," I bark. "There has to be some way to help stave off these infernal side effects. I can't go half an hour without pain when Erin is with me, and it is seriously dampening the mood. How the hell can I woo her when she thinks I'm going to fucking keel over?" My voice is loud and commanding. I get that from my father.

The entire family is silent, and Dr. Mendhi is squirming. "There may be something," he says reluctantly. I want to spit fire. Has he been holding back on me? If so, I am about to lose what's left of my composure.

"What do you mean? Spit it out, man!" my father barks.

Dr. Mendhi's eyes are darting from person to person. I have never seen someone look so uncomfortable. "Well?" I demand.

"Amelia," he begins, but I cut him off. Advancing, I tower over the man.

"Speak, Doctor," I growl.

"There is an experimental serum," he chokes. "It's possible it could help you with the side effects."

"Why the hell haven't you said anything before now?" Lucille hisses.

"Because it's not exactly sanctioned." Doctor Mendhi is visibly shaking now. Not surprising considering he has ten very pissed off Lochs looming over him.

"Illegal experiments?" my mother asks.

The doctor simply nods his head. Under normal circumstances, the Loch family wouldn't be caught anywhere near something illegal, but as I look at my parents doing that wordless conversation thing, I know the lines are about to be stepped over.

My father steps forward. "I don't care what you have to do, Dr. Mendhi, you look after my daughter. Is the serum safe?"

"So far, there have been no serious issues."

"And what is the serum for exactly?" Jacob asks.

"We've been working on a cure for the fallen. To stop the madness."

"A cure?" Mother repeats.

"Yes. However, the elders refused to grant us permission to carry out the experiments needed."

"What experiments?" Aliah asks.

"Experiments on the fallen. Live participants."

Once again, silence falls. We all know what he means. Somewhere out there is a lab with crazed vampires having God knows what done to them. "How can this serum help Amelia?" Marcus has stepped forward, his shoulder leaning into mine. It's a show of support.

"So far the serum can't stop the change, however, we have seen vast improvements in the vampires injected. I believe the serum is powerful enough to stop Amelia's side effects temporarily."

"A bit like an insulin injection?" Maria asks.

"Yes, similar. Amelia would need to have the serum several times a day."

"Well, what the hell are we waiting for?" My mother demands.

"Doctor, do what you must. We want Amelia to have the serum by tomorrow."

He doesn't protest, he just leaves. Turning from the doctor, I face my family. They are all observing me carefully. All except Lucille, who is grinning at me. I scowl at her, and she laughs because she's a bitch. "Why are you staring daggers at Luce? What's she done this time?" Jacob asks.

"No reason," I reply coolly. From the lack of questions, I gather Lucille has not told the rest of the family about my date. But with the look she's giving me now, I know it's about to come to light. God, she is—

"How'd the date go?" Smug doesn't cover how Lucille looks.

"Date?" mother gasps.

"You went on a date? With Erin?" Laurence clarifies.

"Yes, I did." The collective cheers are enough to make me scream. I understand their elation, but they have no idea how far from perfect it was, or how screwed I still am.

"Stop yelling," I shout. "It was a disaster, so you can calm down on the celebrations."

"How the hell did you fuck it up?" Lucille sighs.

"I had an episode in the middle of dinner."

"I bet that was attractive," Lucille deadpans. I have to smirk. She's not wrong.

"Oh yes, totally turned Erin on," I chuckle.

"Explain what happened, love," my father says, pulling me into a side hug.

"What's there to say? I was near her, she mentioned leaving and the next thing I know I'm nearly doubled over in pain. Again."

"What did Erin do?" Marcus asks.

My cheeks heat. Why am I embarrassed to tell them what Erin did? Maybe because it felt so intimate, I don't want anyone else to know.

"She comforted you, didn't she?" Jacob supplies.

"Yes, she did, and the pain vanished."

"Oh, Amelia," my mother coos. "It's going to be okay. I know it." I wish I had her faith. I really do. "When will you see her again?"

"She's working tonight, but then has two days off. I presume she will see Mack." My heart aches knowing that Erin is still spending time with Mack. "We didn't set a second date. Erin was too worried about me." Another punch to the love muscle.

"Then phone or message her. Why are you fucking about?" Ah, Lucille is such a wordsmith.

"She's not wrong," Aliah adds.

I can't believe I'm going to say this. "You know, for once, I agree."

Lucille gives a mock gasp, making everyone chuckle and me roll my eyes. I need to do something now, if I'm ever going to get Erin to look past my health issues. Sending her a message asking if I can have an hour of her time tomorrow puts me back in the running, especially when I get an instant reply saying she would love to see me.

"Done," I grin.

"Let's eat," my mother shouts. It's ten-thirty, but that doesn't matter. If Victoria Loch tells you it's time to eat, you eat.

Date two has to go better than the first date. Dr. Mendhi moved heaven and earth to procure me a month's worth of serum in under twenty-four hours, which makes me believe he is at the center of those experiments.

My moral and ethical compass will have to take a back seat for the time being. My body needs a respite from pain. I'll donate a bunch of money to a charity as soon as I can. Hopefully that will help balance the scales.

Dr. Mendhi was clear that I have to take the serum regularly. My body will become reliant, which I'm not happy about, but what else can I do? He was clear that missing doses would be a bad idea. I did not ask for the specifics. I'm intelligent enough to know it would likely cause either a significant amount of pain, or worse. The injection site has to be my ass for some reason. Guess who volunteered to jab a needle into me?

"Stay still," Lucille growls.

"I am," I reply just as testily.

Lucille gives my ass two sharp slaps. "Just prepping the area," she says.

"You're an asshole."

"An asshole with a giant needle."

Gritting my teeth, I wait for the sharp sting, but it doesn't come. "Done," Lucille announces.

"I didn't even feel it."

"Why do you sound disappointed? Do you want me to really stab you next time?"

"Obviously not." Pulling up my jeans, I turn to Lucille. "Thanks," I mutter. She nods and packs away the serum.

"Have you decided where you're taking Erin?"

"Up the coast on my bike."

"Excellent choice, sister. Beautiful views and you in tight leather. Well played."

"I try."

The weather is perfect for a cruise on the bike. I didn't tell Erin what I planned, so I hope she is pleasantly surprised. Her apartment is twenty minutes away, which gives me plenty of time to settle into the ride.

As I pull up, I see Erin step out of her building. She's wearing jeans and a t-shirt, which is fine. I've brought my spare leather jacket and helmet with me. I can't read her expression. It's a mix of excitement and apprehension.

The door to her building opens moments later and out steps Mack. Given the hour of the day, I can only conclude she spent the night. Now, this is usually the time I start to feel a little unwell. Seems that Dr. Mendhi's illegal vampire juice is doing its job. I barely feel any discomfort.

Mack eyes me with a smirk. Leaning in, she whispers something in Erin's ear and then kisses her deeply. I'm still sitting on my bike. Kicking the stand down, I make a spectacle of de-straddling the seat. Mack might have taken Erin's breath away momentarily, but her eyes are firmly on me. I remove my helmet and run my hand through my hair. That move never fails.

Plastering a smile on my face, I step toward Erin and Mack. "Good morning. Isn't it a beautiful day?"

"Amelia," Mack answers flatly. I take it she's no longer pretending to like me. That's fine.

"Hey, hi, sorry. I thought I had a few more minutes." Erin is flustered. She's looking between me and Mack.

"No worries at all. I'm a little early. The traffic wasn't as bad as I thought."

"It's fine, so, um, yeah, okay, I'll see you soon, Mack." Mack eyes me a second longer before leaning in for another kiss. I chuckle silently. I have to give it to the woman. She's a fighter.

Erin looks utterly uncomfortable. Her eyes keep straying to me as Mack continues the kiss. Finally, after a ridiculous amount of time, Mack pulls back. "See you later, babe."

Erin and I watch her leave. Mack peers over her shoulder and I offer her a little wave. "So, are you ready to go?"

"We're going on your bike?"

"If you're okay with that. You said you've always wanted to try it."

"God, yes, I can't wait."

Pleased we aren't dissecting the show that I was just subjected to, we head to the bike. I help Erin with the jacket and helmet. When she slides behind me and grips my waist, I have to admit it turns me on instantaneously. I think I need some alone time with my vibrator this evening. There is only so much sexual frustration a vampire can take.

Nothing beats a ride, but with Erin on the back, it's perfect. She is a natural, leaning when I lean, shifting her weight when necessary. After an hour, I pull off. There is a beach I love that is usually quiet.

"It's beautiful here," Erin says.

"It's one of my favorite places."

"I can see why."

We fall silent, but it's comfortable. Both of us are taking in the sun, smelling the sea air.

"I'm sorry about Mack," Erin sighs.

"You have nothing to be sorry for. You guys are dating."

"Yeah, but that was a bit much this morning."

"Taking a wild guess, Mack isn't totally happy you're dating me too, right?"

"She said she was fine with it. But, no, after that display, I think she's finding it hard."

"Do you want me to back off?"

"No!"

I grin at how fast she answers. "Are you sure? I don't want to cause you hassle, Erin."

"I like Mack, but I like you too. I've been honest about that. I'll talk to her."

"Don't do that on my account. Really, it doesn't bother me."

"It bothers me."

Time for a little honesty. "I am kind of jealous she gets to kiss you, though." Erin turns away from the ocean to look at me.

"I never said you couldn't kiss me, Amelia."

Bingo! Turning to face her. I take a small step forward. Her chest is rising fast, and I know she's excited. Hell, I'm excited. I can't explain what my body is feeling.

Tucking a strand of hair behind her ear, I let my fingers glide down her jaw, stopping at her chin. Lifting her head slightly, I slowly draw in. I want her to remember this. I want her to see the want in my eyes as we share our first kiss. I want her to feel the raw power of us.

# Thirteen

I've dreamed about that kiss for the past three nights. Nothing in my twenty-nine years has ever left me feeling so high, or full of wonder. Erin's lips are perfect. Soft and plump. They glided with mine effortlessly. The touch of her tongue on my bottom lip had me moaning. I took her in wholly, savoring every caress and lick.

The memory of her hands grasping at my waist sends minor tremors of pleasure to my clit. Three nights I have dreamed and three mornings I have climaxed to Erin. To the memory of that kiss. Although my soul seems temporarily sated, I am still having the serum shots.

"Show me your ass," Lucille barks, barging into my room. I huff and switch off my vibrator.

"Could you knock next time?"

"Amelia, I've heard you masturbating for the last three days. If I wait for you to finish, I'll never get to work."

Rolling my eyes, I shift to the side and poke my ass out of the covers. "Hey Amelia, I have a question." Erin's voice registers seconds before she sticks her head around my bedroom door. "Jesus, sorry."

Wonderful.

"I'm nearly done Erin, just a second," I call. Lucille quickly administers the serum and makes herself scarce. Pulling on underwear, I hurry to the living room.

"I'm so sorry, I should have waited for you to answer, it's just there's a problem with an order and I didn't know how you wanted me to handle it, so I thought I should just ask you, and I knew you were home. That was a bad idea, wasn't it? Are you okay? What was Lucille injecting you with? Is it your ulcer?"

I watch her take a gigantic breath in. That was one hell of a ramble. "Are *you* okay?" I laugh. "That was some speech off of one breath."

"Yeah, fine," she puffs.

"Right. I'm good, thank you. The doctor has given me a new treatment for the ulcer. Unfortunately, it means I need an injection in the ass. As you saw," I smirk.

Erin grins and blushes. "Yeah, I saw."

"It also means that I have to see Lucille more often."

"I could do it," she blurts. Even I'm taken aback by the offer. "I mean, if I'm here. No need for Lucille to stop by."

Lucille moved out of the penthouse several days ago. Her presence is no longer required. Even my mother agreed.

"Well, who am I to pass up an offer like that?" I laugh. "I'll need another jab in a few hours."

"Consider it done." This is a weird situation I find myself in, but I'll take it. What could it hurt, having Erin check out my ass several times a day?

"So, this order?"

"Right, the invoice is way over. I can't find the fault."

"Let me get dressed and I'll be down to look."

There's that lingering again. But now, I'm wondering if it's okay for me to kiss her. I take a chance. Slinking my hand around her shoulders, I pull her in. Our lips meet again and it's just as good as the first time. The only trouble is I have to actively stop my body from trying to take it further. God, I want her. I want to run my hands over her skin, nip her neck, and suck—

"Amelia," she breathes. A pulse of longing wraps itself around my throat, causing me to make a weird little groan. By some miracle, I'm able to pull myself away.

"Sorry," I pant. Erin is on the clock. I have to show some modicum of professionalism.

"No... um, it's fine," she stutters. We are both breathing heavily. Her eyes are black pools. She wants me and I want her, but I know she still has mixed feelings about us. The fact she's still dating Mack is enough proof. I don't want to sleep with her until I know she only wants me. When we bond, I need her to give me all of herself.

Taking a step back, I point to the bathroom. "I'll be down soon." It's not going to be that soon because I'm going to have to take care of myself again.

Forty-five minutes later, I finally emerge from the shower. The number of times I had to make myself come before feeling any relief should embarrass me, but it doesn't. Erin does something to me. She invades my mind and elicits feelings so strong that one climax is nowhere near enough to quench the thirst.

Kit is on bar duty today. It's been a while since we've hung out. I make a note to have a drink with her later. "Hey, everything okay back there?" I ask.

"All good, boss," she calls from below the bar. "Need some more limes, though."

"I'll make sure they are delivered. Have you seen Erin?"

"Yeah, she's in the back. Um, Mack's with her."

"I'll give them a second, then."

"Drink?" Kit asks, already pouring me a Dirty Martini.

"As if you need to ask."

Kit shrugs her shoulders. "It's polite to ask."

I laugh. "How are you Kitty Kat? It's been a second since we had a catch up."

"I'm good, Amelia. The club keeps me busy." I sense an undertone of sadness.

"Hey, what's up?"

Kit sighs. "I'm nearly twenty-five and I still haven't met my mate. I'm starting to worry. No, sorry. My parents are worrying and are transferring it onto me."

"Hey, come on, there's still time. Look at me, I'm twenty-nine and have only just..." I stop dead because I forgot Kit doesn't know I mated with Erin.

"You found her? You've mated?" Kit's excitement is electric.

"Yeah, well, it's a little complicated," I laugh humorlessly, because let's be fair, it's not funny in the slightest.

Kit is cut off by Mack and Erin emerging from the storeroom. Erin is a little disheveled, and Mack is wearing a grin that I'd like to knock off her face. But, because I am the epitome of calm and collected, I don't let her see me rattled.

"I just need to run to the bathroom and then we'll go over that invoice, if that's okay?" Erin asks, her voice pinched. It's not nice to see her uncomfortable. She doesn't wait for an answer.

Mack watches her leave and then turns her attention to me. I already sense what's coming. "Amelia, a word?"

"Sure," I reply, gesturing to the booth on my left. We take a seat. I lay my arms across the back of the booth. I can see it irritates Mack to see me so unaffected by her.

"Look, I think it's time you backed off."

"Really? And why's that?"

"Because me and Erin are exclusive now. We've been together for a few months and, let's be honest, she's only dating you because she doesn't know how to let you down. You know, she feels bad about you having a health issue and all."

My face gives nothing away. My insides are boiling with white fiery anger. "Is that so? Well, until I hear that from Erin, I'll continue to date her."

Mack shakes her head and chuckles. "You poor sap. Amelia, Erin is my girlfriend now. I know you got a kiss out of her, but that's it. You're nowhere near the level we're at."

"Yet."

"No, you'll never get there. Look, if she was so into you, would she have just let me fuck her up against the stock shelves? And boy, did she enjoy it."

Oh Mack, you simple fool. I would be impressed, but I find her as intimidating and threatening as a throw pillow. She oversold it and has just handed me a weapon that is almost guaranteed to blow her relationship out of the water. I'm weighing up whether I should launch it when she leans forward.

"I have to say, hearing her scream my name in your stockroom was quite a thrill." Well, that settles it then.

"For a doctor, you're not very bright, are you?" I begin. She's taken aback by my response. "You know, I really admired you when we met Mack, but you've really shown your true colors now, huh?"

"Hey guys, what's going on?" Erin asks as she approaches the booth. Time to detonate.

"Ms. Hanson," I say, addressing Erin formally, which, of course, earns me a very confused look. "I need you to clear out your locker immediately."

"What?" she blurts.

"I've just been informed you have taken part in sexual conduct on the premises and on shift. As you know, this directly violates your employee contract. I have no choice. Please vacate the bar by the time we open." I have zero intentions of firing Erin. I know Mack was bullshitting the second those words left her lying mouth. Erin would never do anything to jeopardize her career or the bar's integrity.

"What? Amelia, what are you talking about?" Erin is flushed and confused, and I hate that I'm making her feel that way, but it's necessary. If it were any other employee, I would have to take the same steps. I can't be seen as playing favorites, plus I need Mack to know she's fucking with the wrong person. I'm a Loch for Christ's sake.

"Dr. North has just informed me of your time spent in the stockroom. I have to say I'm shocked, Ms. Hanson. Now please, collect your things."

"Mack, what the hell is she talking about?" I stare Mack dead in the eye. She is bright red and panicking.

"No, no, Erin, it was a joke, a miscommunication," she stumbles.

"Odd joke," I comment.

"Joke? What are you talking about?"

"Sorry, can I clarify," I interrupt. "Did it or didn't it happen?"

"It most certainly did not, Amelia. I swear to you." I take a second to look over Erin's beautiful face.

"Right, okay. We'll say no more of it, but in future I think you and Dr. North should keep your liaisons, no matter how innocent, out of Insomnia." With that, I stand and leave.

Twenty minutes pass with no sign of Erin. Kit tells me she escorted Mack out. I get into work mode and trawl through the invoice. I see the mistake and call the vendor. By the time I'm off the phone, Erin is standing in the office doorway looking sheepish.

"Amelia, can we talk?"

"Sure, come in."

"I am so sorry for Mack. I don't know what got into her. I still don't understand how that joke came about. Suffice to say, she will not visit Insomnia as anything other than a patron in the future."

Does that mean they're still dating? "Are you planning on seeing her again? Romantically?"

Erin shuffles in her seat and looks down at her lap. There's my answer. God knows what lies Mack manufactured for Erin to agree to continue dating her. "Um."

"It's fine, Erin. That's your choice." Now I'm about to do something risky. "I think we should put a pause on us until you know where things are going with Mack." I hate myself for saying it, but I need Erin to want me, and only me. I'm wasting precious energy battling with Mack.

"What? Why?"

"Honestly? I can't date you while you're with someone else. I like you Erin, a lot, and I want us to date exclusively. But I know you're not on the same page as me."

"I don't want to stop dating you."

"I'm not the type of person to give ultimatums, Erin. You like Mack, enough to put up with the bullshit she just pulled. And let's not pretend it was anything but bullshit."

"She said it was a joke."

"And you have every right to believe her."

"It wasn't a joke?"

"It was a poor attempt at making me jealous." I'm done playing. Mack is not worthy of Erin's attention. Even if she eventually doesn't want to be mine, she is worth more than Mackenzie North.

# Fourteen

I told Erin she needed to talk to Mack again if she wanted to hear what she really said to me at the booth. Our time in the office was short and awkward, but I meant what I said. If Erin dates Mack after this, I need to take a step back.

Mondays are dark. The club is closed and I'm happy to be doing absolutely nothing. Erin hasn't contacted me for two days, which I suppose should give me a clue as to where I stand with her. It's possible my brain is in shock because the consequences of my gamble haven't hit home just yet.

I'm standing in my bathroom staring at my ass in the mirror, trying to figure out if I should even bother sticking the needle in today. Maybe a good dose of pain will snap me out of my haze.

A deep sigh escapes my entire body. I'm tired and frustrated. If my family finds out what happened with Erin in my office, I will never hear the end of it. I can already hear Lucille's scathing remarks in my head.

*"What the fuck do you mean you told her you were stepping back? Are you a goddamn moron? Of course you are. Why am I even asking? Jesus, Amelia, how are we related?"*

I assume it would be along those lines. Lucille doesn't pull punches. I've spent hours questioning myself. Should *I* have told Erin what Mack said? I could have, but Erin deserved to hear the truth from Mack. They have to sort out their relationship; I can't be in the middle. Well, not anymore.

"Do you need some help?" Erin's voice is usually calming, but I wasn't expecting her and I'm sure I just had a stroke out of fear.

"Shit," I hiss, clutching the bathroom sink with one hand. The needle in my hand is shaking violently. How did I not hear her come in?

"Sorry," she grins.

"Yeah, you look it," I laugh. "Are you like a ninja or something? That's twice you've come into the penthouse undetected."

"I'm light-footed. Anyway, do you... need help?"

"Sure, thanks." I might as well take advantage of her being here. Saves me poking myself in the wrong place.

"You can see where it needs to go." I have several red marks from previous doses.

The injection takes but a second. Erin drops the needle into the biohazard bin stationed next to my bathroom door. "Can we talk?"

I look at her for a second and nod. "Of course. Go grab a drink and I'll be through in a second."

Is she here to tell me she's making a real go of it with Mack? It's likely, I suppose. They were dating for months. Maybe Erin forgave Mack for her indiscretions, and they plan to live happily ever after. If that's the case, I'm catching the next plane to Hawaii and will spend the days I have left with a coconut drink and white beaches.

Erin is sitting on the sofa when I enter. She has a beer in one hand. There's one for me on the coffee table. I sit with her but leave a decent amount of space. "So," I begin, because I don't want to drag this out.

"I spoke to Mack."

"And?"

"She stands by what she said. That it was a joke."

"Okay."

"That was until I told her we have cameras stationed at every VIP booth, with sound." Erin, you crafty kitten.

"And did that influence her story?"

"Considerably. She told me what she said to you. Claims it was her insecurities, and that she's sorry. Oh, and she loves me." Wow!

"Quite the declaration. Should I be getting ready for a wedding invitation?"

Erin laughs. "No. I broke it off." My heart is in my throat. "I can't be with someone like that. And..."

"And?" I am dying to hear these next words.

"I don't want you to let me go." Holy shit! Did you hear that? My soul did because it's doing the Cha Cha Slide right now.

"What do you mean by that, Erin?"

"Do you still want to date me?"

"Yes, but—"

"No buts. Do you want to date me? Just me?"

"You know I do. But—"

"I only want to date you, Amelia."

"Then, I'm all in." I am totally all in. "When can I take you out?"

"I'd like to take you out this time, if that's okay?"

"Completely. When?"

"Now?"

I want to lean over and kiss her, but I won't. This feels like a reset, a clean slate, one devoid of Mack or anyone else. Just me and Erin. We're just about to leave when the dark angel herself swans in. "Mother wants us all for dinner."

"Hey, Lucille, how are you? How's your day? I'm good, thanks for asking." I snark.

"Erin, darling," she purrs. "It's wonderful to see you. Oh, you must come to the house. Mother would be furious if I didn't have you come with us."

"Lucille, we were just about to go out."

"I'll let you call Mom then," she sniggers.

"It's okay, we can go over. I'd like to see your family again." There is nothing but sincerity in her voice and face. Erin is an angel.

"Fine," I mumble, less than pleased our date is being commandeered by my mother.

"I came in the Porsche, so you'll have to find your own way over," Lucille calls, already leaving.

"Bike?" I ask Erin. I know she loved our trip to the beach.

"Yes," she says excitedly.

Well, at least I get to have her anchored to my body for a few minutes before the Lochs kidnap her. I guarantee my parents will whisk her away, trying to pump her for information. Well, Mother will, that's for sure.

We follow Lucille all the way to my parents' house. That woman is a danger to everyone! "Lucille, you are a menace," I screech at her when we pull up. "You nearly took out a parked car. How is that possible?"

"You're so dramatic. Just like Trent."

"No, we're horrified you have a license. For the love of all things precious, let your husband drive from now on."

"Do you see the person you're dating?" Lucille asks Erin. "She has the personality of a cabbage. I hope you know that." I'm about to go all WWE on her, but the touch of Erin's hand on my lower back pulls my attention. I turn to her, Lucille forgotten.

"It's okay. I like cabbage," she says with a sweet smile. One I can't stop myself from mirroring.

"Gross," Lucille mutters.

The door to the house swings open and out sweeps my mother. She makes a direct line for Erin, just as I knew she would. "Erin, how fantastic to see you. Come in, everyone's here." And that's that. I won't get five seconds alone with Erin until we leave. I hope there's alcohol.

The house has been decorated. Floor-to-ceiling. "Is there a party I wasn't aware of?" I call to anyone that will listen.

"Yes," Jacob laughs. "And you're not going to like it," he mumbles in my ear.

"Erin," my mother shouts. It's her way of getting us all to listen. "I'm so glad you came. The dinner today was to discuss you."

"Me?"

"Erin?" I ask. What is going on?

"Yes, a little birdie tells me it's your birthday on Friday!"

"Is it?" I should know this, it's on her personnel file.

"Um, yeah it is," she laughs nervously.

"Well, all this," Mother says, waving her bejeweled hand about. "It's for your birthday party." I groan internally. I knew they wouldn't be able to stay out of it.

"For me? What? Why?"

"Because you're special to Amelia, therefore special to us," my father chimes in. Thanks Dad. Erin looks at me and my very red face. It's amazing how, even as an adult, your parents can embarrass you on the turn of a dime.

"I don't know what to say," Erin stutters.

"Nothing to say. We've already contacted your friends and family." Oh Christ, they've done a deep dive into her personal life.

"My family?" Erin parrots.

"Yes, your mom and dad will stay with us for two nights. We want them to feel welcome."

Erin is nodding along. I can see she is overwhelmed. That's my cue. "Excuse us for a second, please," I say, not stopping to wait for anyone to object. Scooping Erin gently by the elbow, I take us outside. "Erin, I'm sorry about them."

"They did all this for me?"

"Yes."

"Why?"

"Because I like you a lot, and this is how they show their support. It's a lot. They're a lot."

"Wow." Erin sits on a lounger. "You like me a lot, huh?" she smiles.

"Yes, I do. But I think you know that already."

"Hum, not sure. Maybe you could prove it?"

"And how would I do that?"

Erin shrugs one shoulder, her eyes smiling mischievously. I sit next to her, our bodies touching. "Maybe a kiss would prove it?"

"Maybe?" Oh this woman. Two can play that game. I lean in. Her eyes flutter shut, but I don't kiss her lips. Instead, I let my breath tickle her neck ever so gently. I ghost my lips across her skin. The goosebumps tell me how affected she is. Slowly, I make my way to her ear. "I can think of many ways to show you how much I like you," I whisper, and then I pull away.

Erin is in a trance, a very sexy, horny trance. I'd bet all my clubs and bars that if we were within ten feet of a bed, we would be in it, doing very naughty things to each other. A small gasp escapes her perfect lips. And my heart soars.

Then my family does what they do best. Ruin the mood. The shouts and wolf whistles through the French doors catch us both by surprise. Erin laughs and buries her face in my shoulder, which I love. I shoot a murderous glare at my family. They couldn't care less. Great.

"Come on, let's get back inside," I say. It's with great reluctance that I stand and pull Erin up. We were quite happy on that lounger. Ugh, families.

"Can we pick this back up later?" Erin nuzzles her nose into my neck again and ruins my underwear.

"We can sneak out right now if you want," I say, only half joking.

"But I have a party to help plan."

"Are you sure you're okay with it? Don't be scared to say if you're uncomfortable."

"It's a lovely gesture. I've never had a birthday party as an adult, so it's really nice. Should I ask how they got my friends' and family's contact info?"

"Probably not," I laugh. "They mean well. Sometimes they just go overboard."

"Well, as a single child of parents who live hours away, I'm thrilled they went overboard."

"What would you like for your birthday?"

"I don't need anything."

"I didn't ask what you needed, Erin. I want to get you something. We're dating now."

"Oh, of course, sorry. Dating protocol, right?" She's mocking me and I don't care. I want to spoil her.

"Exactly. So as your dating buddy—"

"My dating buddy," she snorts. "Is that what you call yourself?"

"For now," I wink. "So, what do you want from your dating buddy?"

"Just to spend time with you. That would be perfect."

"*That* is a given." Our faces inch forward. I'm so close to her lips, so close to feeling them on my own—

"Will you two get in here? I'm starving," Lucille yells. Erin chuckles, stepping back. She grabs my hand and pulls me to the house.

"Later," she whispers. Does that mean she wants to, you know... take things further or does it mean she wants to flirt a little more, with a make-out session?

Whatever it means, I'm ready.

# Fifteen

No matter how hard I try, I can't stay mad at my family. The joy on Erin's face when she walked into her birthday party was everything. There are a dozen people in my parents' house who I've never seen before. I can only assume they are Erin's friends. Spotting her parents wasn't difficult. Erin is the spitting image of her mom.

The Loch family is spread among the guests, playing their roles perfectly. Erin's parents looked startled when they first arrived, but as usual Victoria and Harlan Loch swept in and worked their magic. Now everyone is laughing and chatting as if they're old friends.

The day is going well, and that's why the universe has decided enough is enough. In swoops Dana. Under normal circumstances, my old friend joining the party wouldn't be a cause for concern, but the look she is giving me tells me my day is about to unravel.

"Amelia darling, may I steal you for a moment," Dana says, not really asking for permission. She's already dragging me away from Erin and her friends. I give Erin a smile and wink, hoping that's enough to make her feel comfortable. It's not escaped my notice that Erin recognized Dana from my birthday party.

When we are safely tucked away in a corner, Dana rounds on me. "Amelia, why the hell are you hosting a party for your bartender?"

"Dana—"

"Since when do you socialize with humans?" she hisses. Until Dana pointed it out, the fact I *am* at a party full of humans didn't even register on my radar. For once in my life, I didn't see a difference in our species. I was just enjoying myself with Erin and her family.

"Some things have changed," I say calmly.

"And those things would be?"

"I mated, Dana."

The news hits her hard, which is bizarre. Dana herself has her mate. We were mere playmates, every so often. "You've mated? With whom?"

"Erin." It's clear by her face she has no idea who that is. The one thing about Dana is, if she has no interest in a person sexually, she barely recognizes their existence.

"Who the hell is Erin?"

"My bartender."

"The human?" she gasps, her hand dramatically coming to her chest as if she's just been shot through the heart. This is ridiculous.

"Yes, Erin is human."

"No, no, Amelia, that can't be right."

"It is, trust me."

"Have you lost your fucking mind?"

"Come back and have that conversation in a few months." I laugh.

"Amelia, you can't be serious."

"Since when do you have a problem with humans? You have enough of them in your bed!" I'm not being cruel, just stating facts.

"Humans are fine for fucking! But mating? No, that's just unnatural."

Her words sting me. This is a side of Dana I have never seen. "You think I had a choice? Do you think any of this is easy?"

"There must be something we can do? A cure or something?"

"Dana, this has nothing to do with you. And frankly, I don't want a cure. Erin... Erin is mine. I am hers. There is nothing unnatural about that and I am hurt that you would say such things."

"Hurt? Amelia, you hate humans," she scoffs.

"I never hated them. I don't trust them. That hasn't changed."

"And how, pray tell, is that going to work with the bartender?"

"Her name is Erin. You may have your opinions, Dana, but do not disrespect her in my presence again."

Dana is sufficiently chastised. I see her visibly back down. "I apologize. It's a shock."

"Me with a human or me finding a mate?" It's occurring to me that Dana is feeling jealous. She knows our trysts are over.

"Both, I admit. I'll miss our times together."

I wish I could say the same. Sex with Dana was fun. It scratched an itch. But, if what I feel with Erin pre-sex is anything to go by, I know when we bond physically; it is going to be indescribable.

"Can I meet her?" Dana places her hand on my arm. It's a friendly gesture, but I know Erin has just witnessed it and she is pissed. I don't need to see her to know.

Slowly, I pull my arm free. "You can. But Dana, she doesn't know about us yet."

"What do you mean?"

"Vampires."

Dana studies me for a second and then bursts into laughter. It's loud, obnoxious, and causing people to pay attention to us, which I don't want. "Dana, pull yourself together," I growl.

"Are you fucking kidding me?" she howls. My patience is running thin. I can feel Erin getting anxious. Taking Dana by the arm, I escort her to the garden, far away from prying eyes and ears.

"Stop," I boom. The tenor of my voice pulls Dana up short. She pales before nervously straightening herself out. Being one of the most influential and affluent vampire families holds sway. There is a social hierarchy that I am at the top of. Dana, whether or not she likes it, knows not to cross me.

"Amelia, I'm sorry."

"Have you any idea the stress and anxiety we as a family are going through?" It's a rhetorical question. "Not only have my parents and siblings been through hell thinking I would never find my mate, but they also now have to help me navigate uncharted waters. We have no idea if I'm still going to descend into madness when I turn thirty. I'm already suffering crippling side effects because my soul hasn't been satisfied. My bond with Erin is tentative and yet, I know in my heart I cannot live without her. Don't you dare come here and give me your unwarranted opinions on something you have no idea about."

"Amelia," Dana sighs, her hand finding mine. "I'm truly sorry, you are right. I was out of line. I had no idea what you've been going through. Please tell me how I can help."

"Just be a friend, Dana. A loyal and supportive friend."

"Always. I swear."

"Amelia?" Erin is standing a few feet away, her eyes bouncing between me and Dana and our clutched hands.

"Erin, come here," I say, dropping Dana's hand and extending it to her. "I'd like you to meet my good friend, Dana."

"Good friend, huh?"

"Oh, I like her already," Dana grins. "She's got spunk."

"What I lack in height I make up for in scrappiness," Erin comments. I'm not entirely sure she's even joking. The thought of Erin fighting Dana for me is highly arousing.

"No need for scrappiness," I chuckle.

"No, indeed. Amelia was just letting me know we are strictly friends from now on."

"Good," Erin nods. "Now that's all sorted, are you coming back to my party?" The question is directed at both of us. It seems Erin doesn't hold grudges.

"Lead the way you feisty little minx." Dana has no boundaries, I swear it. Erin chuckles and takes my hand.

As we rejoin the party, Erin opens her presents, of which there are many. My parents have gone way overboard, and Erin is a deer in headlights again. I don't think she's ever seen so many sparkling jewels in her life.

Although everything is going well again, I can't get the conversation with Dana out of my head. More to the point, the part where I confessed Erin doesn't know about vampires. Now we are dating, exclusively, I have to tell her.

But how? Really, how am I going to explain such a massive thing? This will change Erin's view of the world forever.

There is also a gigantic possibility that even if she believes me, the very idea of being with a vampire will be unthinkable. Then what? My thoughts are spiraling. I need air. Excusing myself, I head to my old room. It's only when I lay on my bed that I remember it's been far too long since I had serum injected. With all the excitement of just being with Erin, it completely slipped my mind.

Maybe it's the uncertainty of what's to come that sparks such a violent attack. I curl into a ball, convulsing as pain slices through me. With every ounce of strength I have, I drop to the floor and crawl toward the door.

Erin, I have to get to Erin. Those words play on a loop as I edge closer to the door. When I finally get there, I feel sweat dripping from my face. The sheer amount of energy it is taking me not to pass out is mind-boggling. But I know I have to stay awake. I have to get close to Erin.

At the top of the stairs, I pause, desperately trying to catch my breath. Dragging my body along whilst feeling my insides are being shredded by broken glass isn't fun.

Wheezing, I continue to haul myself along. My only option is to crawl on my stomach down the stairs. I'm going to frighten the life out of people, but I have no other choice.

I'm halfway down when the coughing begins. Crimson liquid paints the step in front of me. My hair hangs down, shrouding my face. If this wasn't such a dire situation, I would find it highly amusing. How much like a Japanese horror story must I resemble?

My eyes search feverishly for Erin. There are people everywhere. None of whom have noticed me. But then I see Lucille look up. Her eyes grow wide, and she sprints away from the person she was talking to. Her sudden movement causes people to turn my way. There is a collective cry of shock. Lucille screams my name as she runs to the stairs.

"E-Erin," I gasp. Blood is collecting in my throat. I can hardly breathe. Lucille reaches me in seconds, followed by my father. I feel him lift me up. "Erin," I wheeze again.

"I'll get her," Lucille shouts, already heading downstairs.

"It's okay, honey, you're going to be okay." Cradled in my father's arms, I give in to the pain. A piercing scream echoes through the halls. It's all I can do to keep myself conscious.

Father lays me on my bed. I can feel my body shaking and I know that if Erin doesn't get to me soon, I won't walk away unscathed this time. Just as I feel time has finally run out, Erin barges into my room, her face ashen.

"Amelia," she cries. Her body slams into mine as she takes me in her arms. The pain ebbs but doesn't disappear this time. I know I need to be closer. With my shaky hands, I cup her face. Tears are streaming down her face as I draw her in for a kiss. If she's repulsed by the blood, she doesn't say. I feel her lips connect with mine. I feel all those wounds stitching themselves back together inside my body.

This has got to be freaking Erin out, but she shows no outward signs. Instead, she continues to kiss me. Eventually, we both have to come up for air. Her lips are smeared with my blood. Good Lord, it's like a slasher movie in here.

A commotion at the door pulls my attention away from Erin. Dr. Mendhi rushes towards me. My mother takes Erin by the shoulders, gently pulling her out of the way. My hand instantly tries to grab her, pull her back, but I'm too weak.

Erin is enveloped into the center of my family, who are crowding the hallway outside my room. I see Aliah take a tissue to Erin's face, trying to clean her up. All the time, that beautiful woman never lets her eyes stray from me. Dr. Mendhi is listening to my lungs and heart. I hardly notice. Everything I am is solely focused on Erin.

Time has run out.

# *Sixteen*

A raised voice stirs me. My body aches and my head is pounding. Slowly, I open my eyes. The scene in front of me is... Well, I don't know what it is. Erin has her back to me. She's standing at the foot of my bed. Hands on hips, legs slightly apart. She's in full protection mode. In front of her are ten tall Lochs and one Dr. Mendhi. The raised voice is Erin's.

"Don't tell me this is an ulcer, because I will reply, you're all full of shit!"

"Erin," Mother pleads. I wonder how long this standoff has been going on.

"No, Victoria. I'm not stupid. This is more than a stomach ulcer."

"It isn't an ulcer," Lucille states.

"Lucille," my father warns.

"No, she's right. Enough lying. That said, it's up to Amelia to tell you the truth."

"Erin," I rasp. Ugh, my throat feels dry, and I can still taste blood. You'd think that with me being an avid drinker of the red stuff, my own blood wouldn't bother me, but it does. Erin spins round. She's next to me in a second.

"Hey, how are you feeling?"

"I'm okay, I promise."

"That's horseshit. Don't spout crap just to make me feel better. I saw you, Amelia." Gone is her fear. Now she is back to the little firecracker I first met. I prefer to see her that way.

"Fine, I feel like crap." I give her a brief grin, which does absolutely nothing to puncture her ire. It's inappropriate timing, but she's turning me on again.

"What's wrong with you?" Her question is direct, her gaze fierce.

"I'll tell you; I swear. But not now, please." I'm in no fit state to be having this conversation. She studies me for a second longer before nodding, her shoulders dropping.

"Can I have a minute alone with Amelia, please?" Dr. Mendhi asks.

Erin reluctantly agrees and leaves with the rest of the family. After that display, I don't have to be worried about Erin not holding her own. I don't know many *vampires,* let alone humans that would stand up to the whole family the way she just did.

"You skipped doses," Dr. Mendhi says. He's not asking.

"I forgot," I say weakly.

"And you almost killed yourself because of it. Amelia, the serum, will only help for so long as it is. Being this close to Erin but not sealing your union is going to catch up to you, and soon."

"I hear you. I'm going to talk to her."

"Do it quickly. That was a severe attack. I honestly don't know if you'd survive another one."

"Well, it's better than going slowly crazy, I suppose," I say deadpan. He doesn't find me amusing.

"Rest for the next day or two. Doctor's orders. I have given you enough serum for the next four hours. After that, you must go back to regular injections. You mustn't miss a single dose. I thought I was clear with you before?"

"Yes, I promise, I'll take it."

"Okay. I'll leave you to sleep for a little while." He moves from the bed but pauses. His face registers some amusement. "You've got yourself a live one there, Amelia," he grins.

"Ha, you're telling me."

My mother is the next person to visit. She looks a little worse for wear. "How are you, love?"

"Could be better."

"No waiting, Amelia. You have to tell her."

"I know," I sigh. "Let me get stronger first. I think I'm going to need the energy to get through this in one piece."

"She never left your side. I know there is a lot to discuss, and I doubt the path forward will be an easy one for you both, but Amelia, there is no doubt in anyone's mind that she doesn't feel the way you do. Or is at least getting there. I imagine she's still confused by her feelings but... my, my, she gave us all a good dressing down. I was a little scared, if I'm honest." I laugh at my mom's startled face as she relives whatever Erin put them all through.

"I told you she was a fiery one."

"Indeed. Erin wants to come in. Is that okay?"

"Yes, please."

Mother leans over and kisses my head. "I love you, Amelia."

"You too, Mom."

I take a few calming breaths. Erin dashes into the room, climbing straight onto the bed. My heart already feels lighter. She takes me in her arms, which aren't that big. We must look a strange sight. Me being so much bigger, nestled in her tiny frame.

"You scared me, Amelia," she whispers in my hair.

"I'm sorry." I should also apologize for kissing her with blood oozing out of my mouth.

"Claire is back now. I called her."

"What time is it?" Erin is still in her birthday dress. "How long was I asleep?"

"Three hours."

"Erin, I'm so sorry. I ruined your birthday."

"No, don't bother."

"Don't bother?"

"Feeling guilty. I loved my birthday, but it's nothing compared to your health."

"Still."

"No, enough!" I'm having mistress fantasies. Erin would look superb in black leather. "I'm staying with you until you feel well enough to go home."

"Get comfy then, because I'm about to fall asleep." Erin wiggles herself into a better position. She is so comfortable. I breathe in her cherry smell and let myself fall just a little more.

For three days and nights, Erin stays by my side. Having her hold me through the night increases my healing substantially. Now, though, she is getting irritated with me. She wants me to tell her the truth, but I'm not ready.

"Okay, you've finished brunch and you've had an hour sunbathing," Erin begins, her tone curt. We are still at my parents' house. "You're obviously feeling better, so it's time to talk."

Sitting up from my position on the sun lounger, I prepare myself. "Okay." Erin seems a little surprised I've agreed. "You're right. I don't have an ulcer. I do have a..." What? Disease? Virus? "...health issue that is rare. The injections help but aren't a cure."

"Is there a cure?"

"Not as yet. But Dr. Mendhi is positive he is close."

"Why do I feel you're still lying to me?" Christ.

"Erin, I know I scared you, and I can't promise I won't fall ill again. But I don't want our relationship to be all about it. We've gone on a handful of dates. I want to concentrate on that, on us."

"I'm not going to push you, Amelia. But, if you want there to be an us, you have to trust me."

"Please trust me that, in time, I will tell you everything. Please, Erin, just let me have this time with you." I scoot closer to her, my face pleading.

"Fine," she grumbles, but it's playful. I smile widely, taking her face in my hands and kissing her breathless.

"Want to take a nap with me?" My voice is silky smooth. I have no intention of napping. My libido is through the roof.

"Are you trying to take advantage of me, Ms. Loch?" God, I love it when she says my name like that.

"Well, we've had three dates. Aren't you supposed to put out now?" That earns me a smack upside the head.

"That's no way to charm a lady into bed, Amelia."

"How about the floor? Couch? Oh, kitchen worktop. You wouldn't believe the things I could do to you on that!"

Her eyes widen and her nose flares. Yeah, she's as turned on as me. We've been fighting this for a while now. I'm almost positive that if I hadn't had that unfortunate bloody episode, we would have been with each other physically that night.

"Where are your *many* family members?" she asks against my lips.

"They took the boat out for the day," I reply, taking her bottom lip between my teeth.

Erin moves with such speed I'm almost bowled over. Straddling my thighs, I hold her close with my hands planted firmly on her ass. The kiss we share is far from sweet. It is demanding and forceful. Clearly Erin is as frustrated as me.

We're only dressed in bikinis, so stripping Erin down to her delicious skin will take me seconds. However, I want to savor her, trace every inch of her body as she pushes into me, her pussy seeking purchase through her scanty swimwear.

Erin has her hands in my hair. The gentle scrape of her nails is driving me wild. Slowly, I guide us down to the floor. Making our way to my room isn't an option. It's too far away and I'm losing control. In one swift move, I rip off her top, causing her breasts to spill out. They are perfect and ready to be in my mouth. My tongue has a mind of its own, as do my hands. As my fingertips skim over her ass cheeks, my mouth devours her left nipple.

"Christ, Amelia, touch me," Erin whimpers. I'm having too much fun sucking on her nipples and massaging her ass. "Amelia," she groans. There is something stirring in me. A frenzied energy I can feel building from my toes.

Shifting, I tug her bikini bottoms off, throwing them to the side. My ears are buzzing. I can only see Erin's body, only hear her breathy moans. My world has narrowed to an Erin-shaped pinpoint. My knees are on fire from the hard floor, but it's nothing compared to the avidity I have for Erin's pleasure. I want her dripping down my face as she writhes.

Her nipple pops from my mouth as I travel lower, grazing my teeth down her stomach. My hands leave the curves of her ass to slide up the back of her thighs. As soon as they reach her knees, I open her wide. The moment deserves a second of silent reverence. Erin is spectacular. Her soft wet folds glisten under the Californian sun. My eyes drift from her pussy up her abdomen to her flushed chest.

Sapphire blue eyes penetrate through to my wanting soul. I am helplessly propelled toward her. I take as much of her into my mouth as I can. Erin's hips move in time with my tongue. The hold she has on my hair is painful and I want her to do it more.

"Oh fuck," she pants. I eat her out with an insatiable appetite. The frenzied energy that was building is now a swarm in my head. I'm deaf to the world, even to Erin.

Something is changing. It's like I'm on the precipice of something wonderful, but I can't quite reach it.

The sound of Erin screaming my name hits my auditory senses like a crashing cymbal. Erin's pussy pulls away from my mouth, her hips dropping to the floor. I hadn't realized I'd hooked her legs over my shoulder and had her ass off the floor as I fucked her.

I so desperately want that feeling back, I want to reach out and grab whatever it was I could feel inside. But it's gone, just a ghost of a feeling imprinted on my heart. I'm so disconnected I don't even realize Erin has moved from her spot on the floor. My shoulders are gently pushed and then my senses return. Erin is standing, offering me her hand. I take it because I need her to lead for a while. I feel disjointed. This can't be what a bond with your mate feels like. Maybe because I haven't come, the bond is only half fixed. As soon as I'm on my feet, Erin turns me. She settles herself on the lounger, pulling me onto her.

"On my face," she purrs. With my knees on either side of her body, I make my way up slowly to her head. With a flick of her dainty fingers, she relieves me of my bikini bottoms. I still have the top on, but neither of us seems to care. Erin is already grabbing my hips, pulling me forcefully into her mouth. The pleasure is instantaneous, but the swarm I felt mere minutes ago doesn't return. I ride her face, painting her chin and nose with my flowing excitement. I can feel the orgasm building as I grind harder. My hands grip the back of the lounger, steadying my body as I come.

With heaving breaths, I slide down her body, positioning myself at her side. We hold each other as we regain our composure. Erin buries herself into my side. We have done it; we have bonded physically.

So why does it feel wrong?

# Seventeen

I'm so confused. Surely, I should feel something significant? The entire bonding process literally changes a vampire. Yet two days after I gave myself to Erin, I feel no different.

Erin finally agrees to go home, which, as much as I hate it, I need. It's become too easy to have her next to me all the time, and if I was in a better frame of mind, I would do everything in my power to keep it that way, but I'm not.

With Erin gone, I call a family meeting. I haven't had a chance to tell them about Erin and I bonding. Honestly, I thought they might have been able to tell, but once again, I'm wrong.

My family is sitting at the table waiting for me to speak. I take several gulps of wine to help steady myself. "I need to ask you something, without interruption or comment until I say." My eyes scan every Loch making sure they agree. There is no point trying to talk to them about this if the moment I announce Erin and I fucked they lose their shit and start celebrating. I wish that could happen, but I know there is something amiss.

"We agree, love, say your piece and ask your questions," my father replies.

"I need to know how it felt inside when you bonded with your mates physically." I see my mother's eyes open wide with glee, but my father stops her from opening her mouth with a look. I silently thank him. "I need you to be specific."

Laurence is the first to answer. "Calm."

"Serene," Lucille answers.

Mother raises her hand. "May I ask a question?" I nod. "Have you been physically intimate with Erin?"

"Yes, but I don't think the bond worked." My voice cracks with emotion. What does it mean? Did Erin's soul reject mine? Was it just sex for her and she isn't invested in me?

"What happened?" Jacob asks.

"We slept with each other two days ago."

"And how did you feel?" Aliah interjects.

"Apart from the usual pleasure, I felt... an energy, something wild inside. I was pleasuring her, and this feeling got so strong I couldn't hear anything but a swarming noise. I couldn't see anything. It was all-consuming. Like I was close to something but couldn't quite touch it. I thought maybe we had to climax together for it to work, but now I don't think that's the problem."

Lucille lets out a snort of laughter. "It doesn't matter who squirts first, you idiot." Her mocking breaks what little control I have left. Instead of the anger that I usually feel towards my sister, I just feel beaten. Tears stream down my face and sobs wrack my body.

The scraping of a chair is the only thing I hear until Lucille's voice is close to my ear. "I'm sorry, Amelia." In all my life I can count on one hand the amount of times Lucille has apologized to me.

"It didn't work, did it," I hiccup. "I can't bond with Erin."

Lucille wraps her arms around me, holding me as I let out days and days of sadness and fear. Finally, I'm all cried out. "I don't think it worked," Lucille whispers. "But I think it will."

"How?" I'm at a loss. Erin and I are dating. We're getting closer every day. We've bonded physically. What else is there? Maybe it's time we all faced the facts that this was always going to be a long shot and now we have the answer. On my thirtieth birthday, I will be an unmated vampire.

"Amelia, darling," my mom softly calls. I lift my head to find everyone looking at me with pain in their eyes. "Have you told Erin who you are?"

"No, not yet."

"Then there is your answer," Maria states. "A vampire's bond has to be physical and emotional. By that, it means giving yourself entirely to your mate. You are keeping such a massive part of yourself from her, there is no way the bond can stick."

"Maria's right," Marcus says. "From what you have described, that wild feeling was your soul reaching out, searching for Erin's. But Erin's soul doesn't know yours yet. The only way to make that happen is to be completely open with her. She has to accept all of you, just as you do her."

"I don't know how to do it," I answer. "When we are together, I could be fooled into thinking she has always been by my side, but then I remember it's still such a short period. I fear the moment I reveal who I am, she'll be gone."

"So, there's two things you're not giving her. The truth of who you are and your trust."

"I think it's fair to say that in the history of humans finding out we exist, it never goes particularly well," I scoff.

"Are you really lumping your mate in with the general human population?" Father asks.

"Amelia, you're scared. You know Erin is the one. Instead of following your natural instincts and primal feelings, you're letting that big brain of yours get in the way." Aliah isn't wrong. Once again, if this was a vampire I was mating with, I certainly wouldn't be in my head about it.

"Tell me how to do this," I practically plead.

"We do it as a family." Mother places both hands firmly on the table as she rises. In full matriarch mode, Victoria Loch has all our attention. "The mating process is yours alone, Amelia. I understand that, but this part? This we can help you with. Breaking such news is going to be hard on you and Erin."

"How do you think she will react?" I can't help but ask. So far, all I have been able to conjure are worst-case scenarios.

"I think she will be naturally shocked and skeptical. However, she isn't stupid. She clocked on to your so-called ulcer quickly. She knows something is going on. I would also wager she is finding her attraction to you confusing."

"Thanks," I joke. The table titters.

"You know what I mean. You are growing close at a remarkable speed, even for lesbians," Mother says, returning the joke. "Erin might be more receptive to the truth if we can explain her feelings towards you."

"Your mother is right, Amelia. Let us do this part together."

"When?" Lucille asks. She's still hovering by my side, her hand on my shoulder.

"Let's set up dinner this weekend."

"Agreed," calls Laurence. The rest of the table joins in their agreements.

"Once she knows, you all need to go back to your lives, wives, husbands and children," I say.

"We return to normal when you are out of danger," Marcus pipes up. I roll my eyes playfully.

"Any idea how we open the conversation?" Jacob asks.

"Yeah, it's not like we can just casually tell her there are vampires in the world," Maria chuckles.

"We need to approach it factually. Dispel all the garbage spouted out by idiot humans," I say.

"Maybe not calling her race idiots, might be the first thing we address." Lucas laughs. "Remember, you are mating with one. You're going to need to really overhaul your attitude towards them."

"I'll try," I grin.

"Try hard. Remember, it's things like that which will keep you from being with her fully. As much as Erin has to accept you entirely, you must do the same."

"I'm sure we've had this discussion before," Jacob sighs.

"Well, we'll have it again and again until Amelia gets it through her abnormally thick skull," Lucille states.

"Okay, so, Family Loch, we're all set for Saturday as the day we come out," Lucas laughs.

I laugh along with them all, but there is no amusement inside my head. Not when I could lose Erin forever, in just a few short days.

"How are you?" Claire asks. It's T-Minus two days until I spill all my secrets to Erin. She and I have spent every night together, wrapped up in sweaty limbs. Erin's appetite for sex rivals my own, or it's just that we can't get enough of each other. On the surface, I have been my usual self. Erin hasn't seemed to catch on to the river of anxiety that flows through my veins as the time counts down.

I returned to Insomnia and the penthouse after the family meeting. Immediately, I filled Claire in on everything that occurred and what was to come. As usual, she is my rock, giving me space when needed, but never too far away in case I crumble.

"I'm okay today. Although ask me in a few hours and we'll see." My fear and anxiety levels seem to peak and trough through the day. One second I feel excited, almost hopeful about telling Erin; it will be a weight off all our shoulders. But then in an instant, I see doom and catastrophe. I'm just thankful the serum is still working.

"Only a few more days, sweetie, and either way, you'll be moving forward."

"Not if she leaves," I laugh.

"Yes, even if she leaves. At least you will have a direction. Right now you're just stuck in limbo waiting."

"Yes, but I'm having fantastic sex in limbo. If she leaves, the sex leaves too!" Claire swats my shoulder, laughing. Making jokes and laughing at my dire future outcome is one way I'm stopping myself from curling up into a ball and rocking until Saturday arrives.

"You're too much," she laughs.

"Who's too much?" Erin chimes next to my ear. Her voice is a melody that plays my clit to perfection.

"Your girlfriend," Claire laughs. That's the first time anyone has used the term to describe us. My eyes dart to Erin, to see how she reacts.

"She's never too much," Erin chuckles, kissing my cheek and squeezing my ass. Okay, so she didn't object to the label. That's great. Or did she just dismiss it? Damn, I need to clarify that before my brain latches on to another negative connotation. I cannot live under another black cloud. I already have enough.

"Girlfriend, huh?" I say under my breath. Erin is still close to my face.

"Too soon?" she asks.

"Nope, just wanted to make sure I have permission to shout it from the rooftops."

"You *are* too much," she laughs.

I take her hips and pull her close to me. "I'll show you too much later." Our mouths crash together, the kiss turning urgent in seconds.

Claire clears her throat, laughing. "Jesus, calm down, you'll set the sprinklers off. Plus, Ms. Loch, there is no fraternizing on shift. Your rules."

I mock glare at Claire but release Erin. "Fine, I'm going to the office to look at spreadsheets."

"Is that your version of a cold shower?" Claire asks.

"Yes, and if that doesn't work, I'll do the staff rota," I laugh.

Hovering by the door that leads to the office, I watch Erin for a few more seconds. I need to soak up as much of her as possible before Saturday. If I can memorize her smile, her laugh and the way she looks at me, I might just make it through Saturday, because I'm pretty sure the looks she'll be giving me then won't hold the same adoration.

"Will you go?" Claire shouts. I salute, shooting a wink at Erin. Settling at my desk, I skim the files and folders littered about. There are plenty of things I should do, but my focus is shot.

Now and then I shoot a glance at the security monitors. I like to keep an eye out for any troublesome customers, but tonight I want to see my girlfriend. I could close my eyes and sense her, but tonight I need to see her.

What I don't need to see is Mack North leaning across the bar talking to Erin. Before I allow myself to indulge the jealousy curdling my stomach, I remember my mother's words. I have to give Erin my trust. With that, I turn away and continue to work.

# Eighteen

Saturday has arrived and I'm a walking stereotype. Picture every brooding vampire ever depicted in literature and film and there you have it. Erin is sleeping soundly in my bed, and I'm sitting with one leg crossed over the other in a chair opposite, simply watching her.

The sun is ascending and soft rays dance across Erin's face. My mind has been a mess for days, and sleep has eluded me. I've done my best to hide my current state from Erin, and for the most part, I think I've been successful. The handful of times she quizzed me, I blamed my mood on work.

The image of Mack talking to Erin in the bar is still etched in my brain. My mother's voice echoes again in my ears, telling me to give Erin my trust. That's easier said than done, especially when I'm about to reveal something to her that might send her running for the hills, or into her ex's arms.

Sitting here is only amping up my anxiety. I rise from the chair and gently place a kiss on Erin's temple. If I'm to get through today without a nervous breakdown, I need to find some peace. There is only one way for me to do that.

Leaving a note at the breakfast bar, I head to the garage. My bike is sitting there just waiting for me to take her out. Traffic is minimal at such an early hour. I have no place in mind. I just need to feel the rush of the ride.

Further down the coast, blue and red lights distract me. Glancing in my side mirror, I see the police car cruising behind me. Pulling over, I hop off the bike and remove my helmet. Dana steps out of the car. She has a tired smile; I presume she has been on shift all night.

"Hey, early for a ride, isn't it?"

"Couldn't sleep," I reply. Dana has been true to her word. She's only expressed support and has allowed me to vent some of my worries over the last several days.

"Want to grab breakfast?"

"Sure, meet you at Bennie's?"

"I'm right behind you."

Bennie's Diner is twenty minutes away, but it's worth the ride over. The pancakes are to die for. Over the years, Dana and I have used it as a place to decompress.

We sit in our usual booth with our usual order of coffee and pancakes. "Long night?" I ask.

"Yeah, too long. I think I'm ready for a change."

"You mean give up the badge?"

"Yeah. David makes enough money for the both of us, and then some. I'm tired, Amelia. Tired of all the bullshit that comes along with the job."

"What would you do? I can't see you sitting around all day, Dana."

"We've started discussing a family."

Placing my cutlery down, I give Dana my undivided attention. Dana and David enjoy their freedom. This is the first time Dana has hinted at settling down with kids. "Is that something you want?"

Dana nods. "Lately I've been feeling broody. David loves kids, and I think we're in a good place."

"I'm happy for you both. Truly, I think you'll make fantastic parents."

"Thank you, sweetie," Dana replies, squeezing my hand. "Now, do you want to talk about the real reason you were driving your bike at the ass crack of dawn?"

"My mind won't shut off. I've tried everything, but today... today is probably going to be one of the biggest tests of my relationship with Erin. It's also going to determine my future."

"That's a lot to process. What's your gut telling you about Erin and her reaction?"

"I don't know if I can trust my gut. That's the problem." I laugh mirthlessly. I've never trusted myself less than I do at this moment.

"Do you want to know what I think?"

"Sure."

"Erin is in deep, Amelia. I know I reacted badly when you told me, but after that, I watched her. She might be human, but she is pulled to you like a vampire would be. Erin may need a few days to let the truth sink in, but I believe she will be okay with it."

"God, I hope so, Dana."

"When is the big reveal?"

"Lunch time. The whole family will be there."

"Have faith in her, Amelia. Don't presume to know what Erin will think or feel. Trust her to love you enough to stay."

"Love me. Dana, we've barely begun dating."

"Timelines aren't relevant in this, you know that. Okay, so you and Erin are a little different, but the feelings are still there. Tell me you don't love her."

"Dana, she consumes me entirely. I can't breathe when I think of her not being by my side. But I understand why I feel that way. What if Erin believes her feelings aren't real, that they're just a manifestation—"

"Stop, Amelia, just stop. If you don't start giving Erin some credit, no matter how she takes the news, your bonding will be unsuccessful because you still doubt her."

We fall silent as I try to wade through the cesspool of thoughts lodged in my head. "I don't want to lose her," I whisper, my eyes slamming shut, trying to stop the falling of tears stinging my eyes.

"You won't. As long as you give her your all, Erin will stay."

We part ways half an hour later. Thankfully, Dana changed the subject and distracted me with tales of her recent calls. The sun is up now, and Erin will be awake. Suddenly, the distance between us is too much. Revving my bike, I set off for the penthouse. I need to make love to Erin; I need us to have that connection before we go to lunch.

Erin is lounging in the bed still when I arrive. She's wearing one of my t-shirts, which drowns her petite body. Her hair is a mess on top of her head, and she's got sleepy eyes. The coffee she's clutching in her hand is slowly bringing her into the world of the living.

"You're back," she rasps, her voice laden with sleep.

"Just a quick ride. Stopped for breakfast at Bennie's with Dana."

"Everything all right?"

"Dana was talking about leaving the police."

"Wow, do you think she will?"

"I believe so." Shucking my clothes, I stalk towards Erin. Her eyes shimmer with want as she scans my naked body.

"Well, good morning," Erin purrs when I reach the bed, taking her coffee cup from her hand.

"Morning," I mumble into her neck. She smells of the sweetest cherries. My mouth explores her skin slowly. Erin's hands caress my back as I maneuver myself on top. Her legs open and I rest my torso between them, feeling her pussy, already wet with desire.

"I want us to come together," Erin gasps as I rock against her.

"Mmmm," is the only noise I can make. Already I'm fighting the urge to climax. Her folds gliding against my own are a sensational delight. I can feel her clit begging for more.

Our pace increases as excitement overshadows control. My hair falls, cocooning us in an intimate world of gasps and moans. Our eyes are locked as our bodies move to the rhythm of our pounding hearts. "Harder," she cries, her body vibrating as I push more. Erin cries out my name, which sends me soaring into oblivion.

"Wow," Erin pants. "That was unexpected."

"I couldn't help myself," I murmur.

"I wouldn't want you to." My head is laying on her chest, I can hear her heart beating. Closing my eyes, I listen and commit the sound to memory.

The Loch house is eerily quiet when Erin and I arrive. The silence is doing nothing to dispel me of the anxiety pinballing around my body.

Taking my hand, Erin stops us just inside the entrance. "Amelia, is everything okay?"

"Perfectly," I reply calmly. "Getting hangry," I grin. Erin's eyes tell me she doesn't believe me.

Rounding the corner to the dining room, we are met with a table of sullen Lochs. "Wow, who died?" Erin mutters.

"Family," I greet.

"Hello, love. Erin, how are you?" Mother asks.

"Very well. Is lunch ready?" The conversation is too polite. Every member of my family looks uncomfortable.

Mother serves lunch, and silently we all begin eating. Ten minutes in and Erin's knife and fork clatter to her plate. "Okay, what's going on? Did someone actually die because this is one morbid lunch?"

My first reaction is to chuckle. I love that Erin doesn't censor herself around my family. But I soon stop laughing when I see every eye now focused on me. Shit.

"We can talk after lunch," I say, earning a scowl from Lucille.

"No, I'd prefer to talk now, Amelia."

Sitting at the dining room table feels far too formal. "Maybe we could adjourn to the sitting room."

"Good idea," Father comments. Without another word, chairs scrape back and the entire clan siphons into the sitting room.

"Erin, why don't you take a seat there, dear?" Mom is pointing to the single seat in the corner of the room. My family squeezes onto the remaining couches. I remain standing, fiddling with my hands by the door.

"I'm seated. Now what's going on?" Erin looks from my family to me expectantly.

I look at my parents, unable to speak. My mother gives me a reassuring nod. Oh shit, here goes nothing. "Erin," I start. My voice is not confident in the least. "There is something I wanted to tell you, but it will require you to be... open-minded."

"I like to think I am anyway," she grumbles. "But, okay, go on, my mind is way open."

"Right, well, okay." Words are escaping me. I wrack my brain, trying to formulate a sentence that doesn't make me sound nuts. "Okay, so... oh, hang on, wait there one second." It occurs to me that maybe I don't have to find the words. In the family office is a record of our family tree, our bloodline. We also keep ancient texts about our species. Maybe if I present them to her, Erin will come to her own conclusion.

I dart for the door, noting the many confused looks pointed in my direction. I don't care. This is the first time I feel confident that I can explain things properly to Erin. The office door creaks open. I hear footsteps behind me. Unsurprisingly, Lucille barges in with a look that tells me she wants to rip into me. I raise my hand. "Luce, just help me," I say, pointing to the texts and books.

Lucille picks up on my train of thought and nods. Together, we collect as much as possible before heading back downstairs. Everyone is exactly where they were minutes ago. Erin is raising her eyebrows at me. I stop in the middle of the room and drop everything to the floor. "Erin," I say, a little out of breath. "I need you to come here and read through all this." I wave my hand over the pile of books.

"You want me to read that?" she clarifies.

"Yes, please. Read it all and then we'll talk."

With a quick glance at my parents, Erin rises from the chair, takes a few steps forward and then drops to the floor. With one more look at me, she picks up a record of our family tree.

Stepping back, I lean against the wall and watch. Erin meticulously reads each document, pausing now and then to look at me and then my family. We are silent as she pours over everything on the floor.

My heartbeat is a runaway train. I watch on tenterhooks as Erin closes the last book on the floor. She stares at the ground for a few seconds before rising to her feet. Turning to me, she regards me silently. I can feel sweat pooling at the base of my spine. "Amelia," she begins, and I am almost sure I am about to pass out. "Are you trying to tell me you and your family are vampires?"

# Nineteen

Clearing my throat, I stand tall and look Erin in the eye. "Yes, that's what I'm trying to tell you."

"And even though I don't think it's the case, I need to ask; this isn't some weird prank you like to pull on new girlfriends, or anything like that?"

"No prank."

"Right." What does that mean? Jesus, I'm nearly hyperventilating while Erin regards me. Her body language is impossible to read. "I'm going to take these books up to your room," Erin begins. "Then I'm going to reread them and sit with the information for a little while. You," she points at me, "are going to stay down here with your family. I need some time to sit with this."

Erin leaves no room for conversation. She has already collected the books and is heading out of the sitting room.

My family looks a little stunned. I stand there, not knowing what the hell to do.

"That went well, right?" I finally choke out.

"I think so," Aliah replies. "She didn't run out of the house screaming."

"Yeah, that's a good sign, sister," Lucas adds.

"So, what? We just hang around and wait?" Lucille asks.

"Yes," Father replies. "Erin has asked for some time. It's the least we can do."

"Let's finish lunch," Mother chimes. I have zero appetite, but I'm not stupid enough to argue. The food sits in my stomach like a bag of rocks. There has been no sound or movement from upstairs. I am fighting myself not to run up there and check on Erin.

"Here," my father says, passing me a tumbler of bourbon. "This might help settle your nerves."

"This is torture," I reply, sipping the amber liquid. I like the burn down my throat.

"It's going to be okay, Amelia."

"I hope so, Dad." The creak of a floorboard upstairs catches everyone's attention. I hold my breath, praying silently that Erin isn't trying to sneak out of the house and out of my life.

"Can you all go back to the sitting room?" Erin calls from the bottom of the stairs. The clock tells me Erin has been upstairs for an hour. Is that really enough time to fully comprehend what we have just dropped on her? *Trust her*.

We filter back to the same spots as before. Erin ushers me to sit in the armchair. I'm clenching everything as she paces back and forth in front of us all. "So, you're vampires."

"Yes," I whisper.

"And from what I've read, vampires have been around as long as humans."

"Absolutely," my father replies.

"Okay, so vampires are real, and you are a family of them."

"Yes," I repeat.

"Sorry, I just need to get this square in my mind. It's a lot."

"Take your time, love," Mother reassures.

"Do you drink blood?"

"Yes, but not human," Lucas pipes up. "There is a lot of misinformation about our species, Erin. We aren't monsters. We're simply different."

"Do you twinkle in the sun?" We all look at her, confused. Erin is trying to keep a smile off her face. Then I understand the reference.

"No, *Twilight* is definitely not an accurate representation of our species," I deadpan. Maria lets out a snort.

"Okay, no disco ball skin, that's kind of a bummer."

Shaking my head, I let myself laugh. "Erin, please forget ninety percent of everything you have ever heard about vampires."

"Okay, so tell me the truth. Why aren't you out in the open?"

"Because of all the lies that have been told," I state. "We are depicted as devil spawn. For millennia, humans have fed their own fears. It would be too dangerous to live openly."

"Yeah, I can see that."

"Ask anything Erin, and we'll tell you." Laurance adds.

"The texts gave me an insight into your history. If I read correctly, Victoria and Harlan, you are over two hundred years old."

"We are."

"Holy shit," Erin mutters. "How old are the rest of you?"

"We are the age, you know," Lucille cuts in. "Well, Laurence and Marcus are a little older."

"This is the part that is a little complicated to explain," Mother begins. I sit back in the chair and allow her to explain how vampires mate. All the time I am watching Erin for her reaction.

"So, at thirty, you change. That is, if you have your mate."

"Put simply, yes."

"And if you don't have a mate?" The family shares a look. "What? What is the problem if you don't have a mate?"

"The stories you've heard about vampires being blood-thirsty monsters," I start. "There is a degree of truth. If a vampire has not bonded with their mate by the time their thirtieth birthday is over, they become those monsters. Our souls are made to find their other half. Once we are bonded, we become immortal."

"Immortal."

"Yes."

"And if you don't, you'll turn crazy?"

"Yes."

"Then what?"

"The family must put you down."

"And by that, you mean?"

"Kill the crazy," Lucille interjects.

Silence descends. "Amelia." Erin's voice quivers and I know what she wants to know. "Have you mated?"

"Yes, I have."

Erin's face pales. "Who is your mate?"

"You are."

Erin stands stock-still, staring at me. "But I'm human. Is that even possible?"

"It's happened a couple of times in the past," Laurence says.

"And they were able to live together?"

"No." Mother drops her head as she speaks. "In each case, the vampire has expired."

"No," Erin barks. "No, Amelia, that cannot happen."

"Before we get into that, I need to know how you feel about all this, Erin."

"How do I feel? Amelia, I have no idea, this is all…"

"Not about this, about me." This is the moment of truth.

"Well, telling you how I feel in front of your entire family wasn't my plan, but okay. I have been drawn to you from the moment we met, even if I was reaming you out for breaking the rules." Erin shoots me a wink. "My feelings for you grew so quickly, it's hard to wrap my head around."

"That's your soul calling for Amelia's," my father says.

"My soul?"

"Yes. We know a vampire's soul is always searching for its mate. This is a strange situation. Amelia has had to fight her urges. There was no guarantee you felt the same, but now, I think it's clear. Your soul has been searching for hers, too."

"When you say fight her urges? What do you mean?"

"The moment my soul mated with you; it craved that bond. If you were a vampire, you would have felt it too and we would have come together, cementing that bond."

"But because I'm human, it's not happening how it should?"

"Exactly. It seems I've had side effects from not bonding with you."

"Are you telling me your so-called ulcer is the result of mating with me?"

"Yes."

"Jesus Christ, Amelia, I am so sorry." I'm out of my chair in a flash. There is no way I will let Erin blame herself for any of this.

"No, stop. This isn't your fault. It's not mine either."

"Mother Nature is a bitch," she sobs into my chest.

"She is," I chuckle.

"So what now? Does that mean we can't bond?"

"We think you can," Lucille adds. "But you have to give yourselves entirely to each other, Erin. This is a commitment of the deepest order. For Amelia, once the bond is set, she cannot live without you, so, Erin, if you leave her down the line, you will kill her."

"Fucking hell, Lucille!" I bark. "Too far."

"No, she's right. But what about when I die?" The wind is knocked out of my body. Throughout this entire mess, I have only thought of what happens to me. Selfish doesn't even cover how I feel right now. "If I understand correctly, the moment we bond, Amelia will become immortal. I won't, so at some point I'm going to grow old and die. What happens to her then?"

"We don't know," I mutter. I'm so ashamed of myself.

"Well, we need to find out," Erin states. "There is no half-assing this, right?"

"We are doing our best to find out. The fact is, Erin, all of this is guesswork."

"We don't even know if you can bond properly," Lucille says. I glare at her because I'm pissed, and it's easy to be mad with Lucille.

"So let's get bonding," Erin grins.

"Erin, you need to take some time and think about this. I don't know how this will change your life, but it will. You need to be one hundred percent sure of this—of us."

"Of course I'm going to think all this through, but, Amelia, now I understand what I'm feeling, I can't even imagine walking away from you." Her declaration should be music to my ears, but once again, I am left deflated. I don't want immortality if Erin can't be with me the entire time. I can't watch her grow old and leave me.

"I think you two need to spend some time together. Talk it out." My father has risen from his seat. "We're here for you both. And, Erin, as far as we are concerned you are a Loch now."

"Just a really short one," she quips, causing everyone to laugh.

Thirty minutes later, we walk into Insomnia. Obviously neither of us are working, but after this afternoon's revelations, we're both in the mood for a stiff drink.

Making our way to the bar, Erin suddenly stops and whirls around, her eyes wide. "Amelia, does that mean everyone here is a vampire?" she whispers.

"The clientele are a mix, but yes, apart from you, everyone who works here is a vampire."

Erin whistles low, "Wow. Even Claire?"

"Yes," I laugh, "Even Claire."

"Uh huh, alright, alright."

"Are you okay?" Erin is taking this remarkably well, so well, I'm a little worried she's going to have a meltdown at some point.

"Yes, just letting it all sink in. Stop worrying." I scoff because that isn't going to happen.

We get to the bar, and I signal Kit. She pours us our usual drinks without asking. Claire enters the bar, smiling as she comes over. "Hello, you two." Erin is staring at her with narrow eyes, which makes me laugh. "I take it she knows," Claire grins.

"You look no different to me, like at all. Nothing would give you away as being a vampire."

"Next time I'll wear my cape and turn into a bat," Claire deadpans.

"Can you do that?" Erin squeals. "I hate bats."

Claire raises a single eyebrow. "Are you being serious right now?"

"No, of course not. I'm just messing. Trying to get Amelia to lighten up. Phew, it's a full-time job."

"Hey," I laugh.

"Let's drink these and go upstairs." Erin necks her drink and is already leaving the bar.

"I'll talk to you later," I call to Claire as I follow Erin to the secret stairs.

Now I haven't got my family with me. I'm feeling a little more nervous. Erin is not having the same problem. We enter the penthouse, and she flops to the sofa, smiling. "It's good to be home," she sighs and my heart thuds. *Does that mean she wants to be here with me? She called it home, so that must mean something.*

"It's certainly been a day."

"Come and sit down."

I make my way over to her. My first reaction is to give her some space, but Erin grabs my hand and pulls me close. Moving, she ends up on my lap, her hands around my neck. "Are you going to kiss me now? It's been hours."

"Do you... do you still want me to?"

"Amelia, I know we have a lot to talk about and there are tons of things you need to explain to me, but at this moment, all I want is the feel of your lips on mine."

Closing the gap, I kiss her with everything I've got. A flicker of a feeling hums in my abdomen. It's not frenzied or chaotic. It's the feeling of hope.

# Twenty

We talk into the wee hours. Erin asks questions, some of which are silly, some not. I answer everything. I leave nothing out. By the time we are both fighting sleep, Erin has learned our entire history.

The smell of coffee wakes me. Cracking open my eyes, I let myself adjust to the light stealing into the bedroom. It's the first time since Erin has stayed here that she is the first one to rise. Sitting up in bed, I stretch my arms over my head. I'm naked, but not because we had sex. It didn't seem appropriate last night. There was too much to go over.

"Morning, sleepyhead," Erin calls. She walks in carrying a tray full of delicious smelling treats and, to my utter surprise, a matte black bottle. It's full of red, I already know that. I've kept them hidden ever since Erin started spending time here, but she's obviously done some investigating.

"Morning," I reply, eyeing Erin and the bottle.

"So, we have toast, fruit and yogurt, cereal, croissants, and this," she gestures to the bottle.

"Um, thank you."

"It's important you drink it, right?"

"As much as water is important to you."

"Okay, so drink, eat, and then we'll talk some more."

Erin climbs back into bed and starts nibbling on a croissant. I can see her side-eying me as I reach for the bottle. Instead of looking disgusted, Erin seems intrigued. Unscrewing the lid, I take several deep pulls. It has been too long since I've had a drink.

With my thirst quenched, I eat some granola with yogurt. I've decided not to push Erin, but to wait for her to come to me with questions. The one thing I have learned about her is that she needs time to digest information.

"What does it taste like to a vampire?" Erin already knows we only drink animal blood.

"Water, I suppose. There is no real taste."

"Can I taste it?" I'm visibly taken aback by the question.

"Um, if you really want, but I'd hazard a guess it will taste metallic to you, just like your own blood."

"Probably, but I'm interested."

Handing over the bottle, I continue to eat my breakfast. I can see Erin from the corner of my eye sniffing the liquid. Unperturbed, she takes a small sip.

"It doesn't really taste of much, you're right." That's strange.

"Really?"

"Yeah, I mean, there is a bit of a metallic taste, but not much."

We continue breakfast, and I finish the bottle of red. It's going to be so much easier keeping myself hydrated now Erin knows. "What do you want to do today?"

"That's what I wanted to talk to you about." Erin moves the breakfast tray to the floor, then snuggles closer to me. "After everything we spoke about, I think it makes sense that I move in here."

"What?" *Don't get overexcited Amelia!*

"Yes. I can't see you collapse again, Amelia, and we both know that's likely to happen the longer I'm away from you. So, until we bond, I want to be here."

As exciting as that sounds, I'm a little disappointed. Erin moving in should be a celebration of our feelings, not a precaution for my health. "Sounds like a plan," I reply with a smile.

"I know that look," she chides. "I'm not simply moving in because of your health, Amelia. I want to be here with you. It feels right to be here."

"Erin, you're not responsible for me. You have to understand that. This, us, can't be forced."

"Do you think I'm lying about how I feel?" Erin's eyes turn fiery. "Amelia, I might not have the primal instinct to find my soulmate like you, but that doesn't mean my feelings are less. Regardless of all the bullshit, we found each other."

"I'd love for you to move in, Erin. Nothing sounds better, I just don't want to... I don't know, I don't want to mess up your life."

"Amelia, you're pissing me off."

"What? Why?"

"You're acting like my being with you isn't my choice. It most definitely is. Actually, that I'm choosing to be with you should be an enormous fucking clue how I feel about you."

Erin is now out of bed, standing with her hands on her hips, glaring at me. I do the wrong thing and smile because even though she's seriously mad at me, I'm enamored by her passion.

"Are you actually laughing at me right now, Amelia Loch?" Lunging forward, I scoop her up and drag her back to bed. My mouth meets her neck and I kiss her all over. Erin's fire is doused as she giggles under me.

"You're right, I'm sorry, Erin. If you want to be here, I want that, too. I want everything with you. No more doubts. What you say goes."

"Glad we got that sorted," she mumbles into my neck. "Now," she continues, pushing me back. "I wasn't finished talking."

"Sorry," I laugh, holding my hands up in surrender. "Please go on."

"Yes, as I was saying, I want to move in. As for us bonding, I don't think we should rush it. I know there is a time limit, but like you said, it can't be forced. I don't want us spending every second worried that we're not bonding. I also don't want our sex life to become that either. When it happens, it happens."

"Agreed."

"Good. Now, as for today, we're going back to your parents' house for a family meeting."

"Another one?" I groan.

"Yes, because there are way too many unanswered questions for my liking. We need to band together and come up with a plan of action."

"You're very sexy when you get all mistress on me, you know."

"Ah, something you like, huh?"

"Very much."

"Maybe I'll show you my whip one day?" Erin winks at me. Whip? Is she being serious?

"Whip," I cough.

"You're so cute," she giggles. "I'm going to take a shower. You can join me if you like?"

As if she needs to ask that!

Two fantastic orgasms later, we hop out of the shower, dry, and get dressed. I can't believe I have to go to my parents' house again. I don't think we've ever spent so much time together.

We arrive and the house looks like a military war room. "What is this?"

"Erin called this morning and told us to get ready. This is us getting ready," my father chuckles. The dining room table is cleared of all place settings. Books and scrolls are laid out meticulously. Each one with a member of the Loch family poring over them.

"Have you had breakfast?" Mother shouts over the din.

"I fed her up, Victoria," Erin replies.

"Good girl. Right, let's have some coffee and get to work."

"What work are we getting to?" I ask, amused. The whole scenario is surreal.

"Yesterday you told me about a legend or tale, one about a vampire mating successfully with a human," Erin answers.

"Yeah, but it's just that Erin, a myth."

"Nope, I don't think it is. We all know most myths and legends have some grain of truth to them. I think this is the same."

"Why?"

"Because in all the thousands of years vampires and humans have coexisted, I find it doubtful there has never been a match between the two species."

"Have you found any proof?" I know I sound like I'm trying to shit on her theory, but truthfully, I'm scared to get my hopes up.

"I think *I* have," Marcus calls. "I've been wading through folktales all night. The tales are from all across the globe. Usually different countries have different versions of the tale, which in this case is true, but there is a common thread. Every tale talks of a raven-haired vampire born of the original, who fell in love with the human daughter of the first human."

"Maybe," I mumble. "Or it could be bullshit and just a story that got passed down."

"I'm going to smack you," Lucille announces. "It's not solid proof, but fuck Amelia, it's a start. Get off the negative train and start helping out."

"Lucille's right," Erin adds. "Buck up, we have work to do."

My eyeballs feel like sandpaper. If I have to read another old scroll, I'm going to drown myself in the pool.

"I need a break," Jacob whines. "I can't see straight anymore."

"Hear, hear," I call. Slowly I get up from the table. My back is on fire from the position I've held for too long. "Oh Christ, I'm going to need a chiropractor after this."

"Amelia, it's injection time," Erin calls.

"Great," I groan. Walking towards Erin, I stumble. A pain shoots in my chest. Erin is next to me in a flash. Without asking, she draws me in close, pulling my head down, kissing me with abandon.

"Did that help?" she whispers against my lips. I nod. "Okay, let's get you medicated."

We've got the whole injecting me in the ass thing down. Minutes later, we rejoin the family. "I think it's time we bring in the council," my father says. "I know we wanted to keep it in the family, but they have access to more information."

"Will the elders be pissed we kept it from them?" Laurence asks.

"We didn't. Your father and I spoke to a few people we are close to, remember? The Grand Master is still unaware, but I don't think we can keep it from him any longer."

"Will Amelia be safe?" Erin asks, with no thought of her own safety.

"Yes, Erin, don't worry."

"Unlike humans, we don't punish vampires that are different," I snap.

"Whoa there, slugger, what's with the attitude?" Erin laughs.

"Amelia hates humans," Lucille unhelpfully supplies.

Erin rounds on me. "Is that true?"

"No, I don't hate humans, but I have some issues." Honesty is the best policy, right?

"So, you have an issue with me?"

"Honestly, I did when I first found out you were a human."

"Wow," Erin scoffs.

"Will you hear me out?"

"Sure, go for it." Erin stands with hands across her chest. This woman does not give one tiny fuck that she is surrounded by much larger vampires.

"Over the millennia, humankind has demonized us. So much so that we can't live in the open as our true selves. My dislike for humans is out of fear and a need to protect my family. I know not every human is the same, and since meeting you, Erin, I know I have been shortsighted. I have behaved the way I accuse humans of behaving.

"When we held your birthday party, I didn't even realize that most of the guests were human. It was only when Dana pointed it out I understood how silly I'd been to tar every human with the same brush. Sometimes I still get a flare of irritation, especially when I'm reminded of all the terrible things humans have said and done, but I'm sure you would, too, if our roles were reversed."

"Probably," Erin conceded.

"I don't hate your kind, Erin. I just need some time to adjust and unlearn some things."

"Fine, I'll give you that, and I know humans are pretty shitty most of the time, but we're not all bad."

"I know," I say softly, pulling her into a hug.

"Right, let's cut the soppy shit and get back to it," Lucille barks.

"I'm going to call Mohan," my father announces. "I think we should prepare for a visit from the Grand Master."

"I'll cook," Mother shouts excitedly.

"Victoria, we're not hosting a soirée," Father laughs.

"We might as well turn it into one, Harlan. It's been ages, and what better way to introduce Erin to the elders?"

"Elders plural?" I ask.

"Why not? Mohan will need to consult them and the council. We might as well get it all over and done with in one fell swoop."

"I'm ready," Erin states.

"Of course you are, dear," Mother coos. "You're a Loch."

# Twenty-One

As my father predicted, Mohan, the Grand Master, deemed it necessary to visit. My mother has been on Cloud Nine all week planning her soirée. It's quite nice to see her relaxed and excited for a change.

In fact, everyone, including myself, is looking forward to a night of good food and drink. I can't remember the last time I got dressed up. I'm very much looking forward to seeing Erin in a gown. Well, I think she'll be in a gown. She's so far forbidden me from looking at her outfit.

The house is adorned with Mother's finest decorations. Caterers and waitstaff have been hired for the event. Every vampire in a hundred-mile radius has been invited. Erin didn't flinch when she saw the guest list.

"Are you nearly ready?" Lucas asks from my door. Erin and I stayed at my parents' house all this week. Considering we've all had our noses in books for most of the time, it made little sense to keep trekking back to Insomnia. Claire is back in charge. Erin convinced me to step back, knowing we need to concentrate on finding out as much information as possible about the possible vampire human mating told through stories of old.

I'm still not convinced the folktales hold any water, but I've held my tongue. I only upset Erin when I say something, and that's the last thing I want to do.

"Almost," I shout. The black jumpsuit looks great on me. It's one of my favorite and sexiest outfits. My hair hangs down as usual, and I've gone full vamp goth on the eye make-up. "Is Erin down there already?"

"No, she's holed up in Maria's room. I think they're pre-gaming if the giggles coming from the room are anything to go by."

"Oh Jesus," I laugh. Let them pre-game. As long as Erin is having fun, I don't care. "What about Mohan? Do we have an ETA?"

"Twenty minutes. Father wants you to be downstairs waiting when he arrives."

Donning my heels, I give myself one last look over before heading downstairs to the party. Music plays softly throughout the house. My mother and father look every bit the host and hostess. Lucille and Trent are already dancing together.

"Amelia, it's good to see you," Misha Limone says. Misha is the CEO of a large real estate company.

"Misha, it's been too long. How's Lilian?" Lilian is Misha's wife.

"Fat, her words, not mine," she laughs. "She's only got a week left and is thoroughly over the whole pregnancy thing."

"Poor woman. Send her my love, won't you? I need to find my father. I'll catch up with you later."

Wandering to the bar area, I see my father grab two flutes of champagne. "Here, this is for you," he says.

"My hero," I laugh.

"Feeling alright?"

"Fine, I just hope Mohan has some useful information. I'm worried that if we don't find something soon, Erin is going to flip."

"When I spoke to him, he seemed to think he might have something." I nod and take a sip of my drink. "Ah, there he is. Shall we?"

Following my father, I'm grateful Erin isn't downstairs just yet. If Mohan has bad news or no information to give, I get a few minutes to come up with something to tell Erin.

"Amelia, it's wonderful to see you." Mohan Chakan has been our Grand Master for over three hundred years. He is short with a kind face. It matches his character. There is a reason we have voted him into position for so long.

"Mohan," I say, air kissing his cheeks.

"Shall we have a chat and then we can get to the party? If I know Victoria, the food is going to be phenomenal."

"Of course," Father laughs. "You can always count on Victoria." We slip into my father's study. There are already three glasses of bourbon waiting.

"So, I think I have something. After our phone call, Harlan, I went digging in the archives. I believe your theory that the legend holds truth is correct. I believe I found the vampire."

"The vampire that successfully mated with a human?" I gasp.

"The one and only," Harlan smiles. My heart is drumming furiously in anticipation. "And it gets better. I know where he is!"

"Good God!" Father barks in surprise. "That's fantastic. Thank you, Mohan." I'm stunned into silence. "Amelia, honey, did you hear that?"

"Y-yes," I whisper. "Oh, my God."

"Where is he, Mohan?" Father can see I'm overwhelmed and is thankfully taking the lead.

"Ireland."

"Ireland?" I parrot.

"Yes, as in over the sea and far away." Mohan chuckles.

"How can you be sure it's him?"

"I can't be one hundred percent, Amelia. But I have a good feeling."

"We have to go," Father states. "We need to talk to him."

"Not tonight, you don't," Mohan grins. "Tonight we have to celebrate, and I have to meet your beautiful new mate, Amelia."

My mind snaps out of its fog as soon as Erin is mentioned. I need to tell her, but I'm going to wait until the end of the party. She deserves to have a night of fun, away from all the drama. "I look forward to introducing you," I smile. Just the thought of Erin lifts my spirits.

"I'll leave all the information I have in here. Come back to it fresh. I think it would be a good idea to make an announcement. No need to hide anything."

"I'm sorry we didn't tell you straight away, Mohan," my father begins. "We didn't want to cause alarm until we had a better idea of the situation."

"No apology necessary, I understand. Now we can work together and find a solution."

"Thank you, Mohan." I hug him hard. His face rests a little awkwardly on my chest.

We exit the study and mingle with the guests. Erin and Maria are still not here. I'm just about to go searching for them when I see the crowd part and Maria waltz in, looking regal as usual. Her midnight blue gown shimmers under the lights. She smiles at everyone and then winks at me. Stepping aside, Maria reveals Erin.

My God, she is radiant. Her hair is swept over one shoulder in all its golden glory. My eyes track her body, which is sewn into an emerald green strapless dress. Although she is in killer heels, she is still smaller than most people in the room, but what she lacks in height, my word, she makes up for in beauty and presence.

Forgetting entirely where I am and the company I am in, my legs carry me over to her automatically. Taking her by the waist, I bend my head, lowering my lips to hers. The kiss is deep, and passion filled. I want to pick her up and take her to bed.

Maria clears her throat several times before pinching my side. I draw back from Erin, still in a world where only she exists. "You look breathtaking," I breathe.

"Wow." Erin blinks several times, trying to recenter herself. I understand, that kiss was fire. "Um, Amelia," she whispers. "Everyone is looking at us." Ah, yes, the party!

Taking a step back, I run my fingers over her waist one last time before turning to the guests. Half are smirking and half look utterly confused. This is a room full of vampires, so the moment Erin entered, they would have smelled her.

Mohan clinks his glass several times. "Well, now seems like the perfect time," he laughs. "First, I want to thank Victoria and Harlan for hosting yet another wonderful event. I think we can all say it's been far too long." The room mutters in agreement. "Tonight is special, though. Tonight, I have the greatest pleasure of announcing Amelia Loch's mate." Chatter immediately erupts, but Mohan pushes through. "As I'm sure you've gath-

ered by that very warm welcome Amelia just bestowed...
Erin, come here, dear."—Erin gives me a confident wink
and makes her way over to Mohan—"This lovely lady is
Amelia's mate, Erin." More rumbling of chatter. "Now,
I'm also guessing you've twigged that Erin is a human."

"Amelia mated with a human?" a man says somewhere
from the back of the room.

"She did, and we are here tonight to offer our congrat-
ulations and aid. We all know this isn't the usual pairing."

"Mohan, there isn't a single case where this type of mating has been successful," Misha shouts, shooting me a sad
look.

"Actually, we believe we have found one. There will be
difficult times ahead, but I believe Amelia and Erin will
make it through. Will you all hold your drinks in the air
and toast the gorgeous new couple." Without hesitation,
a hundred hands rise in the air. "To Amelia and Erin."

"Amelia and Erin," the room chants.

I'm fending off questions left, right and center. It's been
the same way for the past hour and a half. I know people
are worried, but all I want to do is find Erin—who has been
hijacked by Mohan—and dance with her.

"Do you need rescuing?" Lucille mutters in my ear.

"Please," I beg.

"Amelia, I need to steal you for a few minutes." Dragging me a little too hard by the arm, Lucille directs me to the sitting room. I breathe a sigh of relief when I find it empty. Crashing to the couch, I close my eyes, basking in the solitude.

"Care for some company?" An angelic voice paints a smile on my face. Opening my eyes, I look at Erin leaning against the doorframe, taking me in.

"I'd love some, especially if it's from such a beautiful woman."

"Always the charmer, Ms. Loch."

"Come here," I purr. Erin struts over to me. I sit up, patting the couch next to me. Erin ignores me, hitching up that delicious dress. Fuck me. She's wearing a garter belt and stockings. Seductively, Erin lowers herself so she's straddling my lap. "Hey, baby," she whispers.

"Erin, do you know what you're doing to me?"

"Hopefully getting you wet," she grins.

"That happened the moment I saw you in that dress earlier tonight."

"Maybe I could help clean you up?"

I let out a ragged breath. My eyes work up and down her body. She starts gently rocking against me. "Erin," I warn.

"Yes, Amelia?"

"You need to stop, otherwise I'm going to fuck you on this couch."

"Oh no. You have to wait for that." Her hips are still moving. Her hands grasp my face, bringing my eyes up from her breasts. "Later. You can do whatever you want to me."

"Erin," I whine-slash-gasp. My panties are completely soaked. I've never wanted her so badly.

"Tonight, Amelia."

"Then you need to leave," I say seriously.

"We both do. People are looking for you." The hip roll stops, which is a little upsetting if I'm honest. "Kiss me before we go out there."

Oh, it's my pleasure. I kiss her, taking her tongue into my mouth. Licking her lip, I gently bite down. "Now who's teasing?" she mumbles.

"Just say the word and I'll give you anything you want." I'm deadly serious.

"Give me all of you," she replies.

"You have me entirely."

"I love you, Amelia."

Pulling my head back, I look in her eyes. There is a fierce determination staring back at me. "Erin—"

"I love you, Amelia Loch."

"I love you, too. I am yours, from now until forever." The kiss this time is tender, slow, and knowing. Take away all the vampire/human crap, the drama and uncertainty and all that's left are me and her.

"Do you promise?"

"Erin, we have to go to Ireland."

"Um, that's not what I expected you to say," she giggles. "What's in Ireland?"

"The vampire who mated with a human."

"What?" She grabs my face forcefully. "You found him?"

"Mohan thinks he has."

"Oh my God," she screams. Oh my God, indeed.

## Twenty-Two

"Holy shit, my feet hurt." Erin kicks off her heels, stumbling over to the bed. The party went on far longer than I thought it would. Everyone was in the mood though, so alcohol flowed, and laughter rang out. My heart swelled as I watched Erin mingle. She's a natural and had everyone eating out the palm of her hand.

"Yes, I don't think I'm going to be walking far tomorrow."

"Did you see Mohan? That vamp can dance," she giggles.

"Surprising for his age," I laugh.

"How old is he?" Erin is stretched across the bed, her head resting in her hand.

"Old," I say. Mohan is closing in on a thousand years.

"I've got a question about that?"

"Shoot." I fling off my own heels and settle at my vanity.

"Well, if vampires can live forever, how do you not get noticed? I mean, take the Loch family, for instance. You're all noteworthy and gorgeous. You get noticed. How have your mother and father been around for two hundred years with no one clocking on to the fact they've barely aged?"

"It's easier than you think, actually." Placing my last diamond earring on the velvet cushion I swing 'round to face Erin. "In the days where superstition was rife, it was a lot harder. Anyone could be accused of witchcraft, of being one with the devil. In those days, vampires moved a lot, kept to themselves. Now, it's much easier. The world only sees what it wants to see. Of course, we have to make up stories and move now and then, but it's rare that someone looks too closely. Plus, we can blame our youthful complexion on Botox and facelifts."

"But there are conspiracy nuts out there. Do they ever bother you?"

"Sometimes, but rarely. There have been occasions in the past when a human has gone on a hunting spree. Less so nowadays, but it can still happen."

"I can see why you were so wary of us humans."

"But, like you said, you're not all the same."

"I know, tonight isn't the time, but are you nervous about traveling to Ireland?"

"A little, but that's only because I don't want to get everyone's hopes up. Mohan was relatively sure he's found the right vampire, but until we get there, we won't know."

"I have a good feeling about it."

Standing from the vanity, I stalk towards her. "I can think of something else that would feel pretty amazing."

"Oh, yes?"

"Mmmm, now stand up. That dress needs to come off."

Standing, Erin turns her back. I bend forward, planting kisses on her shoulder as I slowly lower the zipper. "You are gorgeous," I whisper. Letting go, the dress falls to the floor, as does my jaw. No bra, and that garter belt and suspenders. Erin is my wildest fantasy come to life.

My hands move on their own to her back. I just have to feel her skin. My nipples are hard. I want her to know what she does to me, so I step in close, allowing my breasts to rub against her.

Erin snakes her hand behind to grab my butt. "You have too many clothes on now."

Remedying that is easy. I flick the straps of my jumpsuit off my shoulders and lower the side zip. The garment pools at my feet. My body is buzzing with need. "Turn around."

Erin turns, her eyes never leaving mine. "Tonight, we hold nothing back," she breathes. I nod, reaching down to scoop her up. Erin wraps her legs around me. Moving slowly, I turn us and lower Erin to the bed with me snuggled between her legs.

"Just you and me," I say, almost to myself. I need a reminder that she is mine. It's just us, together. When Erin told me she loved me this evening, I felt something blossom in my chest. I didn't tell Erin, but I felt it.

Tonight we aren't fucking. Our movements are languid. Our kisses are soft but passionate. I feel Erin everywhere. That sense I developed when we mated is heightened. It's like I can pinpoint her very essence as our bodies connect.

"Inside me, Amelia," Erin gasps. We've been rocking gently together, building the friction. My hands work deftly to unclip the stockings from her belt. Our mouths continue to explore each other. With a gentle tug, I slide Erin's thong down her thighs and off her legs. I'd forgone any underwear this evening, so now we are both naked and already sweating.

As Erin glides her hand down my back, a trail of pleasure follows. Making a little room, I bring my hand to her folds. Gently and slowly I circle Erin's clit. The hand Erin trailed down my back slips between my legs. Our combined groans amp up the pleasure.

Not wanting to tease, I slide two fingers in. Erin is so hot and wet that I have to slow my breathing to stop myself from getting overly excited. "Oh Amelia, oh yes."

"I want you inside me too," I pant.

Wasting no time, Erin slips inside me. As our rhythm synchronizes, and our breaths become more labored, I relish in the orgasm building in my core. When we come this time, I want to be looking Erin in the eyes; I want her to see all the love I hold for her. Damn bonding, damn everything. All that matters is us, here and now.

"Erin, oh yes, I'm going to come."

"Come, my love, come on me." Holy hell, she's the sexiest thing alive. I pump harder and deeper into her. Our foreheads are together and our lips brush. And then it happens.

"Oh, oh yes, Erin, oh God, I love... you!" My voice disappears. Everything disappears. From the immeasurable pleasure comes a wave of tranquility. My mind falls silent, my body weightless. I'm blinded by a kaleidoscope of gold and blue. If I could describe it any other way, I would say I'm experiencing an out-of-body miracle.

"Amelia," my name sounds so far away. It echoes in my ears. This feeling is so potent I don't want it to fade. "Amelia." There it is again, Erin's soft voice calling me back to her.

"Erin," I call. The world is coming back into focus. I feel her warm body against mine, but she's shaking violently. The bedroom snaps into view. Erin is staring up at me, her eyes wide. I'm still fingering her slowly. I slow and attempt to remove my hand, but Erin stops me. She holds me in place as her back arches. Those sapphire blues roll into her head.

My euphoria is turning into a nightmare. Erin is still shaking. Her grip is tight on my body. I need to stop; I need to bring her back. Oh God, is she seizing? "Erin, love," I shout. Prying her hand off my wrist, I take my fingers from inside.

What should I do? Surrounding her body with my own, I whisper repeatedly in her ear how much I love her. Finally, I feel her back relax. Hovering above, I scan her face desperately. "Erin," I choke. Burying my head in her neck, I'm unable to stop the tears from falling. What have I done?

"Amelia." Erin's voice is haunting me. "Baby." No wait, she's talking, it's her actual voice. My head snaps up to find her looking at me, a smile on her face.

"Erin, love, are you okay?"

"Did you feel that?" she whispers.

"Erin, are you okay? Can you sit up?" Erin might look blissed out, but what just happened was not normal.

"I'm too tired," she murmurs, her eyes sliding shut again.

"Shit," I hiss, "Erin baby, I need to get the doctor."

"Mmm."

Snatching a t-shirt from my drawer and a pair of sweatpants, I tear from my room. I know the doctor is here somewhere. Slamming my fist on my parents' door, I curse out loud.

"Amelia, what on earth—"

"Where's Dr. Mendhi?"

"Amelia?"

"The doctor," I choke.

"Guest wing." My mother looks petrified, but I don't have time to comfort her. The guest wing is at the other end of the house. I take off running as fast as my legs will carry me. There are several rooms allocated for guests, so instead of knocking on doors I scream his name. Seconds later, a bleary-eyed Dr. Mendhi rushes out of his room.

"Amelia, what's wrong?"

"Erin, it's Erin."

I don't wait to see if he's following me. My thoughts are focused on getting back to Erin. My bedroom door is still open. Mother is kneeling by Erin's side, brushing the hair off her face. Maybe I should have covered her up, but I didn't think. I just panicked.

"Step aside," Dr. Mendhi orders. "Amelia, tell me what happened."

"We... we made love and Erin, she reacted... I don't know, doctor. I think she seized."

He checks her vitals. Minutes pass and I'm ready to pass out. What did I do to her? "Amelia, it's going to be okay," Mother says. I wish I could believe her.

"You don't know that." I sob.

Waiting is the worst. I just want to scoop her into my arms and make it all better. "Amelia," Dr. Mendhi says, causing me to jump. "Did anything happen to you?"

All I can do is nod. "What's happening, Doctor?" Mother asks sternly.

"They bonded," he states. "I'm not sure of the consequences of that for Erin."

"What the hell does that mean?" I roar.

"Amelia, this is the first time I have seen a human bond and survive."

"You knew Erin might die if we bonded and you didn't tell me?"

"I couldn't know for sure." I lunge for him. How could he not have warned me? I would never have slept with her, never have fallen in love. I would rather suffer a thousand deaths than see any harm come to Erin.

"Amelia," my father roars. All I see is a red mist. My body is pulled away from the quivering doctor. I feel my dad's strong arms trapping my own.

"Let me go," I scream.

"Amelia, stop. This isn't helping."

"I swear, if Erin dies, I will come for you," I seethe. The doctor's eyes widen in fear. As they should.

The bedroom is suddenly a lot more crowded. My siblings are frantically trying to find out what is happening. It's chaos, but then, amongst the noise, I hear her. My head snaps to Erin. her eyes are still closed, but I know she's talking to me.

Breaking free from my father's vice grip, I run to her side, dropping to my knees. Placing my forehead against hers, I calm my breathing and listen. Tuning everything out, I concentrate on her sweet voice. She's calling my name. "I'm here," I whisper. "I'm right here, my love."

"Am-Amelia?" Opening my eyes, I stutter a laugh in relief when blue eyes meet my own.

"Erin."

"What happened?"

"Can you move?" There is plenty of time for explanations. I need to know I haven't paralyzed her or something. Her body slowly wiggles. She pushes herself up, and that's when I remember she's naked with a bunch of people looking at her. Tugging the sheet, I draw it up and under her arms as she moves. I stack the pillows behind her back.

"Wow," she finally says. "That was a trip."

"She seems okay to me," Lucille grins. I shoot a sharp look over my shoulder.

"How do you feel?" I ask.

"Amazing. Amelia, did... did you feel that?"

"Yes, I felt it."

"Did we... bond?"

"Yes." I cup her perfect face in my hands and kiss her softly. My heart is still racing, and my adrenaline is pumping. "But you seized and then passed out."

"I'm not surprised. That was intense."

"Damn, Amelia, who knew you were that good in the sack?" Lucille cackles.

"Out," I bark. "Everyone out."

"Amelia," Erin soothes. "I'm okay." I haven't even checked to see if everyone has left as I ordered. My eyes remain fixed on Erin.

"I thought, God, Erin, I thought I'd lost you."

"No, my love. Just the opposite."

# Twenty-Three

"Amelia, you are driving me crazy!"

"I'm just being cautious."

"I. Am. Fine!"

"Erin, less than twelve hours ago you were seizing in my arms. That is not being fine!"

"Dr. Mendhi has checked me out from head to toe. He says I'm good, and I say I'm good. How about you listen?"

"Dr. Mendhi, pfft, don't say that name to me."

"Oh, calm down. I get you're pissed with him, but let it go."

"Let it go. He withheld extremely important information from me. And you could have died. Erin, I don't think that's something we should simply let go of.

"Okay, fine, stay pissed at him, but please stop hovering over me."

"I'm not hovering."

"You won't let me get out of bed. I'm fine, Amelia. I can walk and talk. Nothing hurts."

"Erin, we don't know what's going on inside your body."

"No, we don't, which is why Dr. Mendhi is going to do tests, but in the meantime I cannot stay bedbound."

"It wouldn't hurt you to rest." Why is Erin not understanding? We have no idea why her body reacted the way it did to our bonding. Instead of being cautious, she wants to act like it's no big deal.

"It will hurt my sanity," she huffs. "Plus, we need to pack for Ireland."

"Oh, I don't think so. You're staying here." I'm expecting Erin to blow her lid at me. However, I'm confused and slightly scared when she laughs maniacally.

Hovering by the single seat armchair in the room's corner, I shift from foot to foot. Erin continues to laugh, but now she's throwing the duvet cover off herself. Planting her feet firmly on the floor, Erin rises in all her small glory. She's still laughing.

Backing up, my legs hit the seat, causing me to sit. Erin approaches, her head shaking from side to side. The laugh is now a chuckle. "Oh, Amelia," she begins. "I think we need to have a chat, my love."

I swallow thickly.

"You may be used to getting your way. Being the boss of everyone is bound to have given you a bit of a God complex. However, let's get one thing straight. You and me—we're partners, equals in life. I'm happy to discuss things, listen to your opinion and compromise. That's a normal thing a partner will do. What I will not do is let you dictate to me."

"I'm not dic—"

"Yes, that's what you just did, and I can understand because it came from a place of love and panic. But, Amelia, I'm my own keeper. I ultimately make my own decisions, for better or worse, I am responsible for me. Just as you are for yourself."

"But Erin—"

"No buts. I've listened to you and taken your concerns into consideration. I have also listened to the licensed medical professional. He's happy for me to get on with life, as am I. We are going to Ireland together because this affects me just as much as it does you, and like I said before, we are partners. If it makes you feel better, we can bring Dr. Mendhi along with us."

"He's useless," I growl.

"No, he is not. Dr. Mendhi is the one who has the most to offer us right now. Build a bridge and get over this issue you have with him. Okay, so he should have said something about us bonding and the consequences. I think you scared him straight."

"He risked your life."

"He didn't know for sure. But this is what I'm talking about, Amelia. We have bigger things to concentrate on. Put your anger aside. We have a plan and hopefully, when we've tracked this super old vamp down, we will have some answers."

The whole time I have been sitting looking up at Erin tearing me a new one, I can't help but fall more in love with her. Erin is so strong, much stronger than me. "I'm sorry, you're right."

"I know I am. Now, I'm going to shower, and then I'm going to pack for our trip." It's on the tip of my tongue to ask if I can join her, but then the flashback of Erin seizing and passing out floods my mind and I stop myself from speaking.

Oblivious to my thoughts, Erin heads to the bathroom attached to my room. She closes the door and I let my head fall into my hands. How am I ever going to make love to her again? How can I put her in that position? Dr. Mendhi has no idea if it could happen again. Hell, we're guessing that the episode last night means that Erin and I bonded. Until I turn thirty, we can't be sure.

"What's with the doom and gloom?" Lucille asks from the door. I really need to start locking the fucking thing.

"Not now, Luce," I say. I'm not in the mood to spar with her.

"I'm not here to bust your balls, Amelia. I came to see if Erin is okay."

"She says she's fine."

"And you disagree?"

"Honestly, I have no clue. Dr. Mendhi says she is okay. Erin says she's okay, but I'm the one that cradled her body in my arms as she seized. That's not okay."

Lucille pushes off the door and heads to the bed. Sitting on the end, she mirrors my pose. "I'm going to say something that you're not going to like."

"What a surprise," I deadpan.

"Yes, but this time I'm not doing it to piss you off on purpose," she grins. "The fact is, Amelia, you catastrophize everything. You see a situation, and instantly think negatively. I know you blather on that you're just being realistic, but that's bullshit."

"It's not," I growl.

"Yes, it is. Amelia, you have been the same way since we were children. This situation with Erin is serious. I'm not disputing that, but you must admit, you've fought it the whole way. Since you met Erin, you have been the one to come up with all the worst-case scenarios."

"Um, look around, Lucille, I was right to worry."

"Worry, yes, but you're doing more than that. I heard Erin just a minute ago. She was right to put you in your place. You can't dictate to her. You can't take this on like it's your problem alone. Amelia, your whole family has been trying to help for years but you've resisted, convinced the worst was preordained. You are making this harder."

Am I?

"I like Erin. She won't allow you to get away with it."

"I'm aware of that."

"Let people in Amelia. Let us help."

"I have!"

"Only when you literally collapsed."

Okay, she's got me there, I suppose. I exhale. My body is wracked with fatigue. I don't think I had a minute of sleep last night. "I don't know what to do, Luce."

"Yes, you do. You're going to Ireland. You'll find this vamp and gather as much information as possible. And…"

I don't like where this is going.

"You'll have us all there to support you."

My head whips up. "I'm sorry, what now?"

"That's the real reason I came up here. Obviously, I wanted to check on Erin but also to tell you that mother has ordered the family to prepare for a trip to Ireland."

"Why?" I screech.

"As I said, Amelia, to help and support. Anyway, it's been ages since the Lochs had a family vacation."

"We all went to Vegas last year," I protest.

"Yes, but we've never been to the Emerald Isle."

"But—"

"Why are you even trying to argue? Mother has spoken, end of discussion. Get packed and make up with Erin."

Lucille flounces out of the room. I hate it when she gets the last word. Scrubbing my hands down my face, for what feels like the millionth time, I take a breath. I need to stop fighting the help being offered. And I know I need to look for the positive in all this. I have to, for Erin.

"Shower's free, babe," Erin calls from the bathroom. I pad over, slinking in just in time to see Erin towel herself off. I don't think I'll ever get used to how beautiful she is. My carnal urge is to get her against the sink and plunge my fingers into her until she screams, but the fear that overwhelms me a second later stops me yet again. I quickly shed my clothes and jump under the hot stream of water.

Erin leaves me alone. Flicking a switch on the panel by the tap, I wait for music to flood my bathroom. My head is a hive of questions, and I desperately need a few minutes of respite.

The soothing voice of Eva Cassidy lulls me into a serene state of mind. I wash my hair and body, feeling invigorated once again. Stepping out of the shower, I let my body sway to the rhythm as I dry myself off.

"My God you're sexy," Erin says. My eyes open to find her grinning at me devilishly as she scours my body, her hunger for me clear in those expressive eyes.

I give her a wink, but nothing more. Walking up to her, I peck her on the cheek and head to my closet. Dressing, I continue on as if nothing is out of the ordinary. Which it is. Before last night, I would have taken Erin up against the door as soon as I spotted her looking at me. Now? I can't do it.

"Are you packed?" I ask.

"No, I literally just got out of the shower," she laughs.

"Well, we best get to it. Apparently, the family is coming along now." I roll my eyes.

"Ah yes, the family that saw me buck naked last night."

Shit, I forgot about that. "I wouldn't worry. I covered you quickly."

"Amelia, I'm kidding. I don't care if they saw my tits. Hell, they're fabulous," she smirks.

"Yes, they are."

"You don't seem too happy they're tagging along."

"You wouldn't be either if you'd ever experienced a Loch vacation."

"Oh, it can't be that bad, surely."

"Ha, you have no idea."

"Tell me!"

"Oh no. This you have to experience."

Erin pulls me in by the waist. I've managed to get a bra, panties, and slacks on. "I'm looking forward to being part of it," she whispers as her lips skate across my neck. My clit twitches and pulses. Her lips are enough to get me off. I know it.

"You are..." I swallow thickly again "... part of the family."

"Good." Her tongue licks the shell of my ear. Erin is driving me nuts. God, I just want to rip her robe off and fuck her senseless.

"We… we should get ready." I pull away, pecking her on the temple. Throwing a jumper over my head, I step away from Erin, who is looking at me with drawn eyebrows. I take my suitcase from the back of my closet and set about ramming the clothes inside.

"Okay," Erin finally says, elongating the word. Of course, she knows I'm acting weird, but I don't have it in me to have that conversation yet. Not when she's just going to tell me she's fine and I'm overacting. Not when she finds out the thought of sleeping with her again scares me to death.

Silently, we organize ourselves. I excuse myself to call Claire and fill her in on our plan. Insomnia will be in her sole care for the foreseeable future. Honestly, I think it's best if I bring Claire on as a business partner, officially. God knows what the hell will happen over the next twelve months. I need Claire to take over my responsibilities. And, in the event I turn into a raving lunatic on my birthday, I want to know my legacy will continue in capable hands.

Is that me catastrophizing again?

# Twenty-Four

"**L**ucille Loch, if you don't stop hitting your brother, I'm going to instruct Nathan to turn this jet around and take us back to LA."

"He started it," Lucille whines, making me titter.

"And I'm finishing it," Mother declares.

Erin's shoulders are shaking with silent laughter. I did try to warn her that a Loch vacation was going to be interesting. So far, we've endured Lucas's snoring. Lucille's attempts to beat Jacob. Aliah's off-key singing and my father's insistence we all partake in travel games. All that and we've literally just taken off. For once, I'm pleased we are using a private plane. The public shouldn't be subject to this.

After I got over the shock of knowing all my family planned to join us on our trip to Ireland, I refocused on keeping my eye on Erin. Everyone gave her a hug when we ventured downstairs this morning. A choir of "how are you" was followed by an "Erin, you have fantastic breasts." It shocked me to hear *Aliah* make the statement, when that was prime Lucille. Before I could admonish Aliah for being crass, Erin spoke up. "Thanks, I grew them myself."

With everyone laughing, including me, we began our epic journey. I say epic because any time I have to spend traveling with all my siblings *is* an epic effort on my part not to kill them after five minutes.

"How are you feeling?" I ask Erin quietly. She rolls her eyes, but at least answers me.

"I'm fine. Just like I was ten minutes ago, and ten minutes before that."

"Okay." I'll drop it for now. Spotting Marcus, I give Erin's knees a quick squeeze and head over to him. Maybe giving Erin a bit of space from me is what's best right now?

"Marcus, you're looking rather thoughtful on your own over here."

"Just thinking."

"Anything you want to talk about?"

"I suppose I'm just psyching myself up for the trip. It's never easy to travel with you lot," he smirks. Marcus and I share a dislike of family trips, for the same reasons. We're all adults and yet revert to adolescent assholes the moment we hang around each other for too long.

"Well, I'm trying to stop Erin from giving me death glares every five seconds, so mind if I sit with you for a while?"

"Ah, you're being overbearing, right?"

"Can you blame me?"

"No, not at all. Honestly, Amelia, I'm not sure how I would have reacted if in your position."

"Well, according to Erin, not well," I chuckle.

"Has Dr. Mendhi done his check-up?"

"Yes, but only after Erin made me leave."

Marcus laughs. "You scared the piss out of him, Amelia."

"I wanted to rip his throat out."

"He should have told you his theory or concerns. But let it be now. He's here to help."

"Mmm, something Erin also said."

"Listen to her. There's a reason she's your mate."

"What does that mean?"

"You've always needed someone to call you on your shit and not let you wallow. Erin is that person."

A smile breaks across my face. I can't help it. Every time I think of Erin and the fact that she is mine, I'm filled with overwhelming joy. "She is, which is why I'm giving her some breathing room. I pissed her off this morning."

Marcus laughs again. "Shocking."

"Yes, well, it wasn't my finest moment. Fear is a great motivator to say and do stupid things."

"It sure is. How are you feeling about Ireland?"

"I just hope it gives us what we want. Mohan only had an address. We might be disappointed by what we find. Erin is upbeat about it—"

"But you're not feeling so chipper?"

"Exactly. Nothing about this mating has been easy. Why should it start now?"

"Because the universe owes you one," he smiles. "If the vamp has moved on, we'll do everything in our collective power to find him, Amelia."

This is what Lucille was lecturing me about this morning. I don't know why the idea of my family's help puts me on the back foot, but I have to stop resisting and accept it. "I know you will, and I love you all for it." The sound of Aliah hitting a high note off-key makes us both wince.

"Even when you have to put up with that?" Marcus jokes.

"They invented valium for a reason," I laugh. We fall silent for a few minutes. "What do you think happened to Erin?" I ask quietly. Marcus has spent more time than all of us studying scrolls and texts. He's also learned as much as he can about our physiology and the change that occurs after mating.

He blows out his cheeks. "It's really hard to say. I'm sure Dr. Mendhi has his theories."

"What are *your* theories?"

"We know that a vampire's soul actively searches and bonds with its mate. As far as we know, a human soul doesn't work the same way, but it's my guess that for whatever reason, and I really don't know how or why, but Erin's soul was almost... what's the word... activated? Awoken? I think her body reacted to her soul reaching out to yours."

My gut is telling me he's on the right track. I need to talk to Erin again. After last night, I was far too worked up to fully understand what she felt. My chin is cradled in my hand, which is resting on the fold-down armrest. "Mm, I think you're right."

"It's a complete guess, Amelia."

"I know, but it's still worth considering. I need to talk to Erin."

"Do it then." Looking over my shoulder, I watch Erin laugh at something Maria has said.

"I'll talk to her tonight when we're alone."

"Do you think his human is still alive?" He, being the vampire, we're looking for. Marcus's question makes my stomach roll. It's the question I've tried to avoid thinking about the most.

"I hope so," I breathe.

"Looking at it from a scientific point of view, I would say she would have to be."

"Meaning?"

"His soul bonded to her. We know that once that happens, one cannot live without the other."

"Riiight."

"If she died, I doubt he would still be alive. At least, I doubt he would still be sane."

"He could have fallen," I say.

"No. Mohan knows all the fallen vampires."

"True." My heart skips a beat. Marcus is talking logically, and for once, the news looks favorable. "I'll ask the good doctor."

"Play nice," Marcus smiles.

"Always," I laugh. Standing up, I look down the aisle. Dr. Mendhi catches my eye but looks away quickly. I feel a little bad now. Erin and Marcus are right. I need to move on.

"May I sit?" Dr. Mendhi shuffles in his seat, looking nervous, but nods. I slip into the empty seat and cross my legs. "Do you think the human is still alive?"

"I take it you mean the human that successfully bonded with the vampire we are visiting."

I thought that was obvious! "Yes, the very same."

"Yes." His answer is confident. "I don't believe the vampire in question would be still here if she were dead."

"You sound sure of that."

"It's a fact that our souls link. The bond cannot be separated."

"But that begs the question of *how* she is still alive."

"Doesn't it just," he replies with a twinkle in his eye.

"Care to share your theory, doctor?"

"Okay. It's my belief that her body must have changed cellularly, like his did."

"But how? Human bodies differ from ours. *That's* scientific fact!"

"Indeed, but like all living things on this planet, evolution plays a part. If it didn't, we would still be fish." He chuckles at his own joke. "It makes sense to think humans and vampires would eventually evolve to allow crossbreeding."

"And you think that's what happened with the vampire and human who successfully bonded?"

"Yes, but until I see and examine her, it's just a theory."

"Thank you, Doctor... And thank you for tending to Erin last night. I apologize for my behavior. Then again, I don't like to have information withheld, so in future..."

"I won't keep anything from you again."

Nodding to end the conversation, I head back to Erin, who is now alone. "Hey."

"Hey to you too. Did you make amends?"

"I did."

"Thank you." She leans over and kisses me sweetly.

"Still enjoying the trip?"

"Oh yes. The more time I spend with your family, the more I love them."

"Huh! It has the opposite effect on me," I grumble. Erin bats my arm playfully.

"What were you talking with Marcus about?"

"Oh, this and that."

"You are a terrible liar. Where's that smooth poker face you had in place when we first met?"

Laughing, I shake my head. "You, Erin Hanson, stripped me of every ounce of smoothness I had the moment those fiery eyes locked on me."

"Really? I wonder what else I could strip you of." Erin's voice is low, only above a whisper. Her hand snakes to the top of my thigh.

"Easy, tiger," I laugh, but it's forced. Erin's eyes squint almost unperceivably, but I catch it. I know she senses there is more going on. "No sexy times with all my family close by."

Erin removes her hand from my leg and crosses her arms over her chest. "Amelia, what's going on?"

"What do you mean?"

"I mean, this is the third time you've looked uncomfortable when I'm making a move."

"I'm not uncomfortable. Well, maybe a little, but that's only because my family is right there." I hook my thumb over my shoulder for emphasis.

"Hum, okay, so when we get to the hotel, you'll be perfectly happy stripping naked and fucking me." Well, she gets straight to the point, doesn't she?

Taking a quick look around to check none of my nosy siblings are eavesdropping, I scoot closer to Erin. "My love, we have plenty of time for sex. It's going to be a long day of traveling. I'm sure we'll both be shattered by the time we fall into bed."

Erin sits up straighter. "I knew it," she exclaims a little louder than I would like. "You're scared to touch me, aren't you?" It sounds like a question, but I think it's more of a statement.

"Of course not," I lie terribly.

"For a smart woman, you are acting pretty stupid right now, Amelia." Well, ouch! "This bonding thing, you know it works both ways, right?" Um, what does she mean by that?

"Meaning?"

"Meaning that if you'd talked to me about last night, I could have warned you I can do that thing, you know, the thing you do with me?" I'm utterly confused. "I can sense you. In here." She points to her chest. "I can close my eyes and know where you are."

"You can?" This has to be proof of Marcus's and Dr. Mendhi's theory, right?

"Yes, and I can also sense when you are lying to me."

Well, shit!

I clear my throat, suddenly feeling parched. "Are you thirsty? I'm thirsty. Let me grab a couple flutes of champagne." I don't wait for Erin to answer. Unfortunately, grabbing two drinks takes me all of thirty seconds to do.

"Are you done chickening out now?" Erin asks, looking amused.

"I don't chicken out," I say boldly.

"Oh, yes you do," Lucille laughs from behind me. I should have known the Wicked Witch of the West would somehow ingratiate herself into my very private conversation.

"If you're referring to the time, you dared me to eat three ghost peppers, then fine, I chickened out. I like to think I'm just not as stupid as you, dear sister. Now would you kindly fuck off so I can talk to my girlfriend?" I hiss.

"Ooh, someone's a little touchy today," she cackles but does in fact, fuck off.

"You were saying," Erin continues.

Downing the entire flute, I face Erin. "I love you, Erin, and as often as you tell me you are okay, I have last night seared into my mind. Every time I close my eyes, I see and feel you convulsing. The thought of that happening again, because of me, is terrifying."

Erin cradles my cheek with her hand, bringing the free one to my heart. "I think it's time to talk about what I felt last night, Amelia."

# Twenty-Five

E rin is looking at me with so much emotion as she holds my face with one hand and rests the other over my heart. "Last night," she begins. "I felt… something beyond euphoric, Amelia. When I came," she says quietly. "I felt as if I left my body."

"I felt that, too."

"It's difficult for me to put into words what happened. The pleasure was so intense. But I think it wasn't just my orgasm I could feel. I know it sounds weird, but it was like your energy was flowing through me, gripping every cell. And then suddenly everything fell silent and calm. I felt so safe. Like I'd come home. Does that sound stupid?"

I shake my head because it sounds far from stupid. Erin is describing everything I felt. "No Erin, it sounds perfect."

"You felt the same?"

"Yes. Which is why it took me a little longer to come back down to Earth. That's when I saw you fitting."

"I heard your voice," she mumbles into my lips, her breath caressing my face, her nose brushing my own. "You were calling me."

"I called your name. I needed you to come back to me," I choke at the mere memory of that moment.

"Amelia, I came back. I never left. If anything, I was so wrapped up in us, in you. We were closer than ever before."

"It scared me, love." I hate feeling so vulnerable. It's not a natural thing to enjoy, right? But with Erin, that's all I feel, for better or worse.

"I know. And I'm not dismissing that, but, honey, you can't *not* touch me ever again! We can't stop living. There is still so much for us to learn as a couple. I'm so excited about that! I know we've skipped a few steps, going from three dates to madly in love, talk about lesbian stereotypes."

I huff out a laugh. "We're stereotypes on steroids."

"But that doesn't mean we aren't still a new couple. I want romance and dating. I want to learn all your habits, even if they piss me off," Erin chuckles. "I want the honeymoon period, where we can't keep our hands off each other, Amelia."

"Trust me when I say I struggle minute by minute not to touch you," I whisper.

"Then please don't hold back. Trust in me and the doctor to know what's best for my health. I won't keep anything from you, I promise."

With Erin's scent invading my senses, I'm struggling to come up with a counterargument. Maybe it's a sign that I should stop fighting and just let go. Be with Erin and put my fear to one side.

"Okay, I'll try. But I can't promise not to worry, Erin."

"Me, too. Don't forget that I know how this could end for you as well."

I sigh out a breath and let my forehead lean against Erin's. "I love you."

"Then take me to a secluded spot on this damn jet and show me."

Thankfully, we are on a business jet that has a bedroom. Usually, that's reserved for my parents when they have long-haul flights, but today, I think we'll commandeer it.

Taking Erin by the hand, I pull her from the seat. I ignore everyone's eyes staring at us, and I ignore Lucille's wolf whistle as we make our way to the back of the plane.

Rushing through the small door, I kick it closed and throw Erin onto the bed. It's smaller than my king, closer to a full-size mattress, but it doesn't matter. I don't intend for there to be much space between us.

Erin shuffles up the bed, her hair ruffled. Without taking my eyes off her, I strip. Thank God I wore sexy lingerie. As Erin said, we're still a new couple. No reason for Erin to get acquainted with my granny panties just yet. Because yes, even the smooth and mysterious Amelia Loch needs comfy underwear.

"Fuck, Amelia, you are something," Erin breathes out. Her eyes are black pools, and she is unconsciously licking her lips. I did well to choose black lace.

"Now you," I say. I want to watch Erin peel those clothes off her sumptuous body. Rising to her knees, Erin undresses. I take a step back and flick the lock on the door. Nothing is going to disturb us.

"What are you waiting for?" Erin smiles. I'm waiting for my heart rate to calm down. Oh, how I wish the bed had a sturdy frame. I would love to tie Erin to it, make her beg until she is ready to come with just the slightest touch. Oh well, I'll have to wait for that. Instead, I step forward and drop to my knees at the end of the bed. Crooking my finger, I beckon her closer.

Erin crawls to me. I pat the bed in front of me. "Sit." Gracefully, Erin swings her legs around. Casually she leans back on her hands, staring down at me. I'm staring at her crotch because I can already see the damp patch growing darker as she becomes wetter.

I want to take my time, but that's proving difficult. Clad in red lace, Erin is a vision and a tease. My hands start from her ankles and slowly glide up her silky sun kissed legs. There is already a slight tremble in her thighs. My fingertips ghost across her skin.

Lifting her hips only a fraction, Erin urges me to remove her panties. I oblige. My eyes track the red lace as I pull them gently from Erin's body, dropping them to the floor. Her legs are already spread, but I want them wider. Tracing back up to her knees, I use my palms to open her wide. Slick folds glisten, and my whole body thrums with anticipation. I know what heavenly taste awaits me and I'm in a rush to savor Erin once again.

Her heady scent is making me dizzy, but I slow down. I want to see all of her, and I want to suck on her nipples. Snaking my hands up and around, I unfasten her bra, pulling it away. Leaning in, I lick my way from her navel to her left breast, greedily taking her nipple between my teeth. The hiss Erin sucks in as I consume her is highly satisfying.

"More," she commands.

Not one to disobey orders, I tongue my way over to her right nipple, giving it the same attention as its twin. Erin is scraping her hands through my hair, tugging it when I suck a little harder.

Releasing her breast with a pop, I kiss my way down to the apex of her hip. With one last kiss, I pull myself away. I need to see her in all her wanting glory. Erin is gripping the bed sheet hard, her knuckles white. Her breathing is erratic and her gaze animalistic. "Amelia," she growls. Shivers run down my spine.

Hooking her knees with my hands, I throw her legs over my shoulders. Erin's top half drops to the mattress with a relieved sigh. She knows I'm about to give her what she wants. The waiting is over.

I place open mouth kisses, with the hint of teeth on the inside of her thighs. For a split second, I am hit with panic as the memory of last night enters my mind. Mentally batting it away, I continue on. My nose brushes through her short curls and I inhale deeply. Is there a more delectable scent than a woman? I don't think so.

Erin is already moving her hips, waiting for my tongue to connect to her pussy. A small grin etches on my face. I could keep her on the edge for a little longer but I'm a little afraid of what she might do. A small laugh escapes my throat. For once in my life, I can safely say I'm not the boss in this situation. Erin is a power bottom, and she instructs me perfectly.

Feeling Erin's hand grip my hair, I lower my tongue, delicately tracing her swollen lips. "Yes," she pants. Yes indeed! I'm in heaven as I continue my gentle exploration. I have the willpower of a saint because all I want to do is bury my face in her pussy, but I want to stretch out her pleasure more.

"Mmmm," I hum because she really is delicious.

"Amelia, please."

"Please what?" I mumble into her clit.

"More," she moans.

My hands squeeze her thighs as I prepare myself. I'm going to eat Erin out and then flip her over and fuck her from behind. My pussy jolts with excitement at the thought. Rubbing my nose through the length of her slit, I slip my tongue into her entrance.

Erin's hips push forward as she invites my tongue in deeper. She is so wet I can feel her dripping down my chin. Swiping up with my tongue flat, I find her clit and suck, taking her into my mouth with vigor.

"Oh my god," she shouts. I'll put up with the ridicule from my family for this. I'll put up with anything to hear Erin scream. My rhythm increases, as does the pulsing between my legs. Erin clamps her legs around my head as the trembling increases in speed and intensity. "Yes, yes, yes," she chants. I watch her back arch and I pray she is okay. I continue sucking until a deep, guttural moan echoes through the room. Erin's body goes still, and I am on top of her in an instant.

My heart is in my stomach, but the sight of her blue eyes and wide smile calms me instantly. She's okay! Oh, she's more than okay. She's pushing my lace panties aside and circling my clit. "Yes," I pant, dropping my head to her neck. God, I need this.

"Roll over." There goes my plan of fucking Erin from behind. The second my back hits the bed, Erin tugs hard on my panties. I laugh when she throws them over her shoulder with a smirk. Instead of unclipping my bra, she pulls the cups down, allowing my breasts to spill out. Simultaneously, Erin fondles my right nipple with one hand and enters me up to her knuckle with the other. The sensation of having my nipple played with and my pussy pounded is out of this world.

My body arcs and writhes as Erin relentlessly plays me to perfection. And then I feel it, the moment she rubs her fingertips across my G-spot. There is no stopping the sound that emanates from my mouth or the shuddering orgasm that makes me flood Erin's hand. *Holy Shit!*

It takes several seconds for the white spots to stop dancing in front of my eyes. "How was that?" Erin asks with a knowing smile. She buries her head into my neck, her body relaxing on top of mine. Circling her waist with my jelly arms, I hold her tight, breathing her in.

"That was unbelievable," I gasp, my breathing still erratic.

"Yes, it was," she sighs. "Does it feel different to you now?"

"It was definitely more intense, I think. How do you feel?"

"The same. Every touch felt... more. That orgasm was..."

"Yeah, it was," I laugh. "You're sure you feel okay?"

"I promise. I only feel good things. Wonderful things."

We fall silent as our breathing evens out. Instead of dread and panic, my mind is clear and light. Peering over to the clock on the wall, I calculate how long we have until we reach Ireland. Six hours remain. I left the arrangements with my parents. All I know is we will land in Dublin and then we'll drive an hour to a place called Mullingar.

Erin's breathing is slow and deep, her body completely lax on my own. Closing my eyes, I inhale deeply, allowing her cherry scent to lull me to sleep.

# Twenty-Six

I leave Erin to wash up in the bathroom. It gives me time to face the family and allow them to get their jibes in. Lucille spots me first and grins. I roll my eyes.

"Good nap?" she asks.

"Spectacular, thanks for asking."

"Oh, calm down," she huffs. "We all put our headphones in the minute you dragged poor Erin away."

I eye her suspiciously. "Did you really?"

"Yes. Believe it or not, Amelia, I do not want to hear you smashing clams with your mate."

"God, you're so crass," I hiss. Lucille laughs.

"We all know what it's like when you find your mate. Trent and I didn't leave our room for days."

Continuing down the aisle, I stop at the table with food piled high. "We'll be landing soon, Ms. Loch. I need to clear this away." Amanda, the flight attendant, says. I grab a couple of croissants and a glass of orange juice.

"It's all yours," I smile. My parents are sitting with Laurence and Marcus. They have their heads bent over a map of Ireland.

"Ah, Amelia dear, good to see you. Where's Erin?"

"I'm here," Erin calls, taking the glass of orange juice from me. I hand her a croissant, too. We worked up an appetite.

"Marvelous. We were just going over the itinerary."

"Isn't the itinerary to go to this man's house?" Jacob laughs, settling on the arm of my father's chair.

"Yes, and that's the itinerary I'm talking about." Mom gets huffy when she's asked stupid questions. "We land soon. There will be a car waiting for us. Once we reach Mullingar, we need to decide if you want to head straight to the address or find a hotel."

"Straight for the address," I say without pause. I have no intention of dragging this out a moment longer than necessary.

"Fine. And if this vampire isn't there?"

"We find a hotel and regroup," Erin answers.

"Did anyone think to call the man?" Aliah shouts from further down the aisle.

"No registered telephone," my father answers.

"Does he live in town or in the countryside?" I ask.

Marcus and Laurence share a smile. "He lives in the countryside. We Googled the address." Why do I feel I'm missing something?

"And?"

"And what?" Laurence answers.

"Have you seen the house?"

"Yup," Marcus chuckles.

"Care to share the joke?" I snap.

"Nope," Laurence grins.

"You know I could just google it myself, right?"

"No, please don't," Marcus pleads playfully. "Just wait."

"Do you know what they're finding so funny?" I ask my parents. They both wink.

Erin places her hand on the base of my neck. "Let them have their fun, babe."

"Are you kidding?" I ask sharply. Marcus and Laurence laugh. My parents grin. Erin looks confused.

The house we are approaching isn't a house at all. It's a castle. A gothic castle. "What's the problem?" Erin asks.

"It's a bit on the nose, don't you think?" I say, scrunching up my face.

"Oh, because of the whole Dracula vibe," she titters.

"Yes. It's gross."

"Was Dracula real?" Erin asks. Whipping my head round, I glare at her, only to see the sparkle in her eye.

"You're funny," I deadpan.

"Oh, Amelia, chill out," she laughs. "Humans have stereotypes, too. Do you know how many times I got called dumb as a young girl because I'm blonde?"

"But I bet you didn't lean into that stereotype," I shoot back. "This vampire has," I say, pointing to the looming building.

"God, I hope he answers the door wearing a cape," Maria laughs.

"Yes, with his hair slicked back." Lucas chimes.

"I just want him to answer the door," I whisper. My father leans over and pats my knee. "No matter what, we won't stop until we find him."

"Question," Erin says, raising her hand. "If this dude is one of the oldest vampires in existence, why isn't he famous or something?"

"Why would he be?" Lucille asks.

"Because he's like number one."

"So? He's just a vampire like the rest of us. Living his life."

"But he's really old," Erin stresses. I understand her curiosity. If humans found the remains of the very first human, it would be a big deal. But for vampires, we expect to live forever. Nothing to get excited about there.

"He is, but so are a lot of other vampires. This is our norm," Father says.

"Huh." Erin stares out of the car window in thought. I turn to watch the castle get closer.

"Are you ready?" Mother asks when the car stops.

"As ready as I'll ever be." I take Erin's hand as we climb out. There are several lights illuminating different rooms of the castle.

"After you," my father says.

Standing tall, I walk hand in hand with Erin to the large oak door. *This guy better not be wearing a cape.* The bell rings several times. It must echo around the entire building. A minute or two passes before we hear footsteps. The door creaks open and a woman smiles at us. She looks to be in her late thirties.

"Hello, can I help?"

I can smell she is a vampire, so that helps the next part of the conversation. "Good evening," I begin. "My name is Amelia Loch, and this is my mate, Erin."

The woman smiles widely and gives me a knowing look. "You're here to see Bartholomew," she says. Am I? Mohan never gave me a name. "Follow me."

I look over my shoulder to the rest of the family, who all shrug and urge me to follow. Erin grips my hand a little tighter.

The inside of the castle is just as gothic as the outside, making me want to scoff and roll my eyes. "Barty," the woman calls. "Visitors."

"Are we expecting visitors?" a man's voice replies from somewhere upstairs.

"No, but you're going to want to meet them."

We enter a large sitting room with a roaring fire. The woman gestures for us all to sit and then offers me her hand. "I'm Anya, by the way."

"It's a pleasure." I then spend a few seconds introducing everyone as we wait for this Barty fellow. Moments later, a tall blond-haired man enters. He is dressed in jeans and a shirt. A vampire, for sure.

"Evening all, I'm Barty."

This is so strange. How do I begin the conversation? "Barty, it's a pleasure," I say. "I'm Amelia, and this is my mate, Erin."

"Oh, wow," Barty breathes. "It's a pleasure to meet you both."

"Do you... Could we ask you some questions?" I still haven't established if this is the right vampire.

"You want to know if I'm the lucky vampire who mated with a human, right?"

"Yes, that," Erin points at him, laughing.

"Take a seat, everyone." We follow Barty's order. Anya scuttles off to pour us all drinks. "To answer your question, yes, I am. And Anya is the aforementioned human."

"But..." I begin, confused. "She smells like a vampire."

"That's because she is one," Barty laughs.

"How is that possible?" my mother asks.

Barty takes a second to study his mate, who is handing out large glasses of Irish whiskey. I chug mine as soon as the glass is in my hands.

"Honestly, we don't know," Barty finally answers. Well, that was less than helpful. "Remember that back then. We had no doctors. We were still developing as a species."

"Surely you've looked into it since?" I say.

"Not especially. We were just so pleased to have each other we didn't question it."

"Great," I mumble a little too loudly.

"Not what you wanted to hear," Anya smiles understandingly.

"We were hoping for a little more," Erin replies kindly.

"Barty, Anya, would you be open to having our doctor examine you both?" my mother says, cutting through the melancholy that threatens to settle upon us all.

Barty and Anya exchange a look. Anya nods and turns back to us. "Of course, if it helps."

"Thank you," I croak.

"Dr. Mendhi is waiting in the car. He's been overseeing Amelia since she found Erin."

"You experienced pain, I take it?" Barty asks knowingly. I just nod. "I remember that."

"Me too, like it was yesterday," Anya says, closing her eyes.

"Did you get to the coughing up blood phase?"

"Oh yes," I laugh. "During Erin's birthday party."

"Oh my. I'm sure that caused quite a stir?"

"It wasn't fun," I laugh. Barty spends the next few minutes describing his side effects, and they are identical to my own.

"Did you know the bonding had been successful before you turned thirty? You look fabulous, by the way," Erin says earnestly. To be fair, they are a striking couple for being a few thousand years old.

Anya grins. "It's amazing what good face cream can do."

Dr. Mendhi interrupts us entering the room. His eyes fixate on Barty and Anya. I can hear his scientific brain climaxing from here. My father introduces him and then allows Dr. Mendhi to discuss some tests he would like to perform. Barty and Anya agree to everything, which makes me so grateful I could cry.

"We insist you stay here," Barty says once Dr. Mendhi has finished talking. "We have plenty of space and I'd very much like to get to know you all better."

"That's very gracious of you, Barty. We'd be delighted." Father replies, shaking his hand.

Deciding that the good doctor's test could wait until the morning, we continue to drink fine whisky. Hearing Barty and Anya's stories is a little mind-bending. I can't imagine living through the ages as they have. I've never met a vampire older than Mohan and he doesn't really talk about his past. Probably because it was awful. I mean, can you imagine living through the Dark Ages? Medieval Times? No, thank you.

"I have to ask about the castle?" I say, my words are a little slurred. Damn, the whiskey is potent.

"What, don't you like it?" Barty mock pouts.

"It's very on-brand," I laugh.

"It's the first castle we've ever owned. I know it's a little much considering we're vampires, and it perpetuates all those ridiculous stereotypes." I like Barty more and more. "But back in the day, Anya and I never got the chance to stay in a fancy castle. We were smart enough to stay out of the way. Public scrutiny was not something we wanted back then."

"I can only imagine."

"Indeed. Anyway, we ended up in Ireland a few decades ago, and this place was on the market. We snapped it up, renovated it, and have been happy ever since."

"Why aren't you famous?" Erin asks. "Aside from the fact you are super old—"

"Thanks," Barty laughs.

"You're the first vampire to successfully mate with a human."

"Yes, but for nearly all vampires, that was just a myth. Anya and I just wanted to live our lives together. Bringing attention to the fact Anya was once a human would only invite questions. We didn't want doctors banging on the door, wanting to prod and poke."

My face heats. That's exactly what we've done. "Barty," I begin, but am quickly cut off.

"You being here is different. You're not just asking for our help for curiosity's sake, you're living what we did. For that, we are more than happy to oblige."

"I hope the doctor finds some answers," Mother adds.

"Me too," Barty supplies. "If there is anything in our bodies that can give the doctor a clue as to how this all works, I believe he will find it."

"Would it be possible for Erin and me to talk to you alone after the doctor has finished his tests tomorrow?" There are things I want to ask them without my entire family being present. Plus, I don't want Anya to feel as if she has to tell a bunch of strangers about something very private that happened to her.

"Yes, I think that's wise. However, until tomorrow dawns, we drink!"

# Twenty-Seven

Rolling over, I feel a cold spot where Erin should be. Cracking my eyes open gingerly, I silently wince. We drank so much whiskey last night, I'm surprised I'm not still drunk. Hungover, definitely.

"How's the head?" Erin asks from the doorway.

"Not as bad as I expected," I croak. My voice is raw from all the talking and laughing.

"You and Barty sure put a lot away last night," Erin grins, padding over with a cup of coffee in one hand and a plate of fruit in the other. "Here, drink and eat this."

"My savior," I sigh dramatically, earning a pleasant scoff and eye roll.

"Your savior was the liters of red I had you drink before passing out." My memory is foggy. I remember singing an Irish drinking song at one point, but it's a blur after that.

"Sorry," I wince again. I'm not sure how Erin feels about the whole drinking blood thing yet. Well, not for sure. She's seen me a handful of times, but mostly I try to wait until she's not around.

"It's your liver you should apologize to. Now you have fifteen minutes to get up and get dressed. Dr. Mendhi should be finished with Barty and Anya by then."

"What time is it?"

"Nearly eleven."

"Eleven? Damn," I hiss. I'm usually up and dressed by six, at the latest.

"You can't be surprised," Erin laughs. "We didn't fall into bed until three. Anyway, it's given the doctor plenty of time to do his tests. When you're ready, we will join Barty and Anya in the gardens. It's a beautiful day."

Scarfing my breakfast as quickly as I can, I rush to shower and dress. Yesterday's chat with the two vampires wasn't as helpful as I'd hoped, so my expectations for today aren't wonderful, but if Barty can give us any new bit of information, it's a step in the right direction.

The chatter from the dining hall is animated. All the Lochs are in high spirits. Anya and Barty are absent, but I presumed that means they're still occupied with the doctor.

"Ah, she's alive!" Maria calls over the din. I give a small wave in recognition. The table is filled with food. "Have some brunch, that will cure you."

"Drink this," Lucille says, thrusting a glass of red into my hand. I chug it down, still feeling dehydrated from all the booze.

Erin sits next to Aliah and begins a conversation. I still love to watch her interact with my family. I'm not sure I'll ever get used to how wonderful she is.

Taking the seat next to my mother, I refill my glass. Most of my family have red in front of them. Aliah is drinking hers. Erin doesn't seem to care.

"Are you ready for your talk with Barty?" Mother asks.

"I'm not sure how useful it will be, in all honesty honest. If Barty had any new information, he would have told us last night."

"Maybe, but it's worth hearing his story. And it will be good for you to have someone who truly understands what you're going through."

I nod and continue drinking my red. The tightness in my skull is easing with every drop. "What are your plans for today?" If I know my mother, she has organized something for the family to do.

"We're driving back to Dublin for the day. Unless you need us here?"

"Thank you, but I think we'll be okay. We can have a family meeting tonight to fill you in on any new information."

Brunch continues for another twenty minutes until Barty and Anya join us. I can see the little wad of cotton held in place by medical tape on both of their arms. They wave to everyone, Barty looking no worse for wear. That man can drink whiskey!

"How are we all this fine morning?" Everyone answers in unison, causing a rise in noise that is unpleasant on the ears.

"Right, Lochs. Get your things together. We leave in ten," Mother announces, scraping back her chair. Shooting me a wink, she embraces Barty and Anya as if they are old friends. I silently thank her for gathering the brood and clearing them out.

Erin and I continue to eat and drink as the family bickers and argues all the way out of the castle. My mother issues stern warnings every five seconds. I don't envy her today.

"Well, they're a lively bunch," Anya laughs.

"Can you imagine living with them?" I say seriously.

"Shall we take a walk outside?" Barty inquires. I wonder if he is as keen as I am to get this talk over and done with.

The castle grounds are outstanding. Lush green grass, which has been expertly cultured, surrounds the entire property, only broken by the gravel walkways that snake in all directions. Rolling fields and dense trees are the castle's only neighbors. I can see its appeal, especially for old vampires requiring peace and privacy.

"So," Barty begins. Anya is hanging onto his arm as they walk. Erin has her hand in mine, clutching it tightly. "I suppose we should get down to it, huh?"

"Did everything go okay with the doctor?" Erin asks.

"Oh fine, just a bit of blood and other bodily fluids," Barty laughs.

"It wasn't too invasive, was it?"

"No, don't worry. We said we want to help." Anya reassures.

"I think the first thing is to dispel some myths you've no doubt encountered," Barty continues. "I'm not the son of the first vampire and Anya is not the daughter of the first human. It's all a bit too Adam and Eve for me."

"But you are old," I ask.

"Yes, we are. I'm close to The Big 4-0-0-0," he laughs.

"Four thousand years old," Erin gasps. "Wow, I mean, that's old."

"Babe," I laugh.

"Sorry, I hope I haven't offended either of you."

Anya laughs, "Of course not. It's not like we look it, right?"

"And that brings me to the next thing," Barty adds. "I'm sure Amelia has filled you in on all things vampire, but I'll say this anyway. We found that although the aging process halts on our thirtieth birthday, it can take a few years to fully stop. That's why some vampires look to be in their late forties or fifties."

"Amelia didn't tell me that."

"Sorry, I just wanted to keep to the facts," I shrug.

"Also, the whole immortality thing is optional."

I stop in my tracks. "I'm sorry what?"

"What I mean is, our molecular structure changes and our bodies become immortal, but that doesn't mean we have to live forever. Some couples live a handful of lifetimes and have had enough. I can't blame them sometimes after what we have witnessed over the years."

"So you're telling us, some vampires... kill themselves?"

"You could say that, or you could say they choose when they come to the end of their lives. Humans have a natural end to their time on earth. Vampires do not."

"Amelia, did you know this?"

"No. It never even occurred to me to think about it. As far as I was concerned, every vampire is immortal, and that's that."

"It's a common thought pattern. We're so worried about finding our mate, we don't think about the thousands of years ahead of us," Barty states simply.

"Can I ask about you, Anya?" Erin probes. This is what we really want to know about. How the hell did human Anya become vampire Anya.

"Sure. I met Barty and felt this pull to him. I was only sixteen at the time."

"But you look to be in your thirties now?"

"Indeed. We mated, but my change didn't occur until my thirtieth birthday, just like Barty."

"But the bonding process was carried out years before that, I'm guessing."

Barty nods. "Yes. We bonded shortly after meeting. There was little knowledge about our species back then. Just like humans, we were learning about ourselves. For me, I fell in love with Anya and that was that. I had no clue about the repercussions. We learned later on that our mating was extremely rare, if not the *only* successful human/vampire mating."

"Um... When you mated, did you have any adverse reactions?" Erin asks. Like her, I want to know if Anya seized or slipped into unconsciousness.

"Oh yes," Anya chuckles. "Barty thought he'd killed me." It's strange that her sentence brings me comfort.

"I seized," Erin states. "And then blacked out."

"But you felt the euphoria, right? The connection which bound you to Amelia?"

Erin nods her head. "Then you truly bonded."

"But is that enough to turn Erin?" It only then occurs to me that Erin might not want to become a fucking vampire. *Jesus, Amelia, how self-centered are you?* "Erin, do you want that?"

"I want to be with you." She cups my cheek and looks me dead in the eye. "If I need to become a vampire to do that, then I will."

"But what about your family and friends? You know what it will mean if you become immortal."

"Yes, and I can't say I know how I will feel or what will happen when the time comes to say goodbye to the people

I love. I can only tell you how I feel now and what I know in my heart. My life is with you, Amelia. From now until eternity. My heart is yours and I feel myself becoming a part of you a little more every day."

Wow, okay! I need a second to swallow the lump that is wedged in my throat and will the tears to recede without falling. I don't want to become a blubbering wreck in front of Barty and Anya.

Drawing Erin in, I hold her. The steady thrum of her heartbeat fills me with warmth. "If I could choose to be mortal, I would," I whisper. It's true. I would give immortality up in a nanosecond if it meant Erin didn't have to change.

Erin finally steps out of my arms and smiles shyly at Anya and Barty, who are looking at us in complete understanding. "How long until you turn thirty?" Anya asks. I'm not sure which one of us she's asking. Did I tell them my age last night? God, I hate getting blackout drunk.

"I have several months," I answer. "Erin has three years." Barty and Anya nod their heads in understanding. Even if everything goes off without a hitch on my birthday, we will have to wait years to know if Erin will change. Although, I've already decided, if Erin remains human, I will end my life when hers is done.

"Knowing that we've bonded, do you think Amelia will be okay?" Erin's eyes betray how nervous she feels regarding my change.

Barty puffs his cheeks and wiggles his head from side to side in contemplation. "If I were a betting man, I would say Amelia will complete the change without a problem. Her soul has found and latched onto its other half. From what we know about our kind, that is all that is required for Amelia to become immortal."

I'm certain now our bonding has ensured my immortality. I haven't had a single dose of serum in well over forty-eight hours. I have no signs or symptoms, no bleeding or pain. I am whole.

"My worry isn't for myself," I say somberly. "I just hope Dr. Mendhi can give us some new information. I don't want us to be living on edge for the next several years."

"I wish we could have given you something concrete. Just know that we are here for the foreseeable future," Barty smiles, placing his hand on my shoulder.

"How often do you move?" I ask.

"Every twenty years or so. Although we are secluded here, which is why we've stayed longer. No one pays us any mind."

"Is that what we will have to do?" Erin asks me.

"Eventually. My parents had us all in LA, but we will have to relocate at some point."

# Twenty-Eight

We stay with Barty and Anya for another two days. Dr. Mendhi flies home before us, keen to get his samples under his microscope. Well, I presume that's what he has planned.

Unfortunately, we haven't garnered any fresh information from our new friends after our walk in the garden. Instead, we concentrate on taking a couple of days to relax.

With a promise to visit from both sides, we fly back to LA and back to our lives. With no choice but to sit back and wait, I decide we all need to resume work. Erin and I discuss my house outside the city. In the end, selling is the best option. Erin enjoys working at Insomnia and I'm not about to ask her to give that up to move.

Taking up permanent residence in the penthouse above the club suits me fine. It forces me to get involved in my business. I realize leaving Claire and my other managers to pick up the slack is detrimental to me. I'm a business-woman and I love owning clubs and restaurants. Laurence and Marcus were right when they lectured me on my birthday. I had hidden away in my home with my books.

However, now Erin is in my life, I'm determined to start living again. Granted, the hours are long, and we both work six days a week usually, but we make the most of every second together.

Three weeks after our voyage abroad, my father calls me to set up a meeting with the doctor. Both Erin and I have made a valiant effort at putting the doctor's tests to the back of our minds. We've almost resigned ourselves to waiting for both our birthdays to roll around before getting any concrete answers.

"You look delicious," Erin purrs in my ear as we exit the car and begin walking to my parents' front door.

"You don't look too shabby yourself," I grin wolfishly. I will be stripping her naked the second we have an iota of privacy. I've already noticed my siblings have arrived in force. Their cars are lined up like soldiers outside my parents' home.

Mother asked us to dress up for the evening, which in all honesty I could have done without. If Dr. Mendhi has no news, or worse bad news, the last thing I want to do is suffer through a dinner party. But as you are aware, there is no refusing Victoria Loch.

Classical music echoes through the house. I can hear my family chatting and laughing. A part of me wants to rip into them for acting so casually. For me and Erin, tonight is stress and anxiety dressed up in dinner jackets and ball gowns.

"Ah, there you are. My, my, Erin, you look beautiful." I want to scoff and say, "Of course she does, she always looks beautiful," but I don't. Erin accepts the compliment from my mother as well as a tight hug. We make the rounds and hug each member of the family. It really is a dinner party, considering my sisters- and brothers-in-law are also in attendance. I guess my nieces and nephews are watching a film or playing somewhere.

"Mother," I say a little testily. "Did we really have to make tonight such a big deal?" I ask in a low voice.

"Yes, because it's not just about you, Amelia," she says. I look at her, trying to gauge what the real reason is for the Loch gathering.

My father breaks the chatter with a few sharp raps on his champagne flute. "Settle down, you rowdy lot," he chuckles. "Thank you for being here. It's always lovely to have all my children in the house." He gestures for Mother to join him. "Your mother and I have an announcement."

I watch my mother subtly place her hand on her stomach, and then I know. My face breaks out in a wide smile. I catch her eye and she winks. "What are you smiling at?" Lucille barks. Her pissy attitude makes me smile more. I thoroughly enjoy being in the know when my irritating sister isn't.

"If you shut up, you'll find out," I snap.

"Dear Lord, I can't believe we're going to do this all over again," my father half chuckles, half huffs.

"What does that mean?" Lucille bites. Wow, she's in a mood this evening.

"It means we're pregnant," my mother replies. Her eyes are shining, and I can honestly say she is glowing with happiness. I peek to the side and almost choke on my laughter when I see Erin's face.

The rest of my siblings have rushed over to my parents, whereas I hang back with Erin, who still hasn't moved. "Are you okay?" I chuckle. Her rapid blinking informs me she's still processing.

"But... but she's over two hundred," Erin finally whispers in awe.

"Yup, and still very fertile, by all accounts."

"So... vampires can just keep churning out little vampires?" This makes me laugh out loud.

"Well, we're not vampire-making machines, but in a sense, yes. We can continue reproducing. Our aging stops, remember? For Mother and Father, this little one will be no different from when they had Laurence. Mom won't feel any older, nor will my father."

"I just... I mean... wow."

"Does that scare you?"

"What, having a baby when I'm well into my second century? Um, yeah," she giggles.

It's like a rain cloud descends on us both when we realize simultaneously that this might not be our future. I grab her hand and bring it to my lips. Pressing a kiss on her knuckles, I try to convey confidence while channeling my love. "Come on, let's go congratulate them."

We spend several minutes hugging and kissing my parents. I'm thrilled for them both. Dr. Mendhi's appearance at the door interrupts our celebration. Sucking in a lungful of air, I excuse Erin and myself to find out the test results away from my family. I want them to have a little longer toasting the new baby rather than dealing with this.

"Drink?" I ask the doctor as we settle into my father's study. He nods and I pour all three of us a healthy glass of bourbon.

Erin and I sit on the couch opposite Dr. Mendhi, who is sitting in my father's wingback chair.

"It's good news," he says. I rein in my excitement. I've learned not to read too much into people's expressions. Good news doesn't mean we have definitive answers. It could just mean I'm not about to turn into a bloodthirsty monster anytime soon. Instead of answering, I nod for him to continue. "First: Barty is a fine specimen of a vampire. All his tests came back clear. He's had no adverse reaction to mating with a human. Normal on all fronts. Second:

Anya's blood work was fascinating." I find myself shifting closer to the edge of the couch.

"In what way?" Erin asks.

"Anya's blood is a mix between vampire and human."

"How?" I blurt.

"I'm working on it. But, Amelia, this is good, this is progress."

"In what universe? All we have are more questions?" I seethe. I'm so tired of this shit.

"We have more information. Anya's blood is a mix of her own and Barty's." Dr. Mendhi watches us with delight as both Erin and I try to figure out what it means.

"I don't understand," I admit finally.

"Erin, may I take a sample of your blood? To prove my theory, I need to look at yours under a microscope."

"Of course. Can we do it now?"

"Yes, absolutely. I have the equipment." They are rabbiting on and I'm still trying to figure out what the hell it means. How in the world does Anya have a mix of human and vampire blood?

I watch silently as Dr. Mendhi draws Erin's blood. Thinking he's going to pop it in a test tube and file it away in his briefcase, I'm surprised to see him pull out a microscope from his kit. Bustling over to my father's desk, the doctor wastes no time clearing a space and getting to work.

Erin is gripping my hand tight. We wait for what seems like hours as the doctor hems and haws, as he selects different magnifications. I'm almost bursting at the seams when he finally turns around.

"It's interesting." *Interesting! Interesting, is that it?* Erin's hand squeezes me again. She can feel my anxiety and ire reaching its boiling point. "Erin, your blood is still human." I feel her deflation. "However, it has been marked by vampire blood."

"What the fucking hell does that mean?" I cry, making the doctor jump.

"My love," Erin coos. "Sit and listen." She then nods for the doctor to continue.

"At some point, you have come in contact with vampire blood. Not just on your skin, mind you, no, you would have ingested it."

We look at each other for a second, trying to figure out when the hell Erin ingested vampire blood. A look of realization overtakes her face. "When Amelia collapsed on my birthday. I kissed her after she coughed up blood."

"Yes!" Dr. Mendhi exclaims. "Yes, that would explain it."

"But what does that mean?" I ask calmly. I'm doing my level best to rein in my true feelings.

"I believe Anya had a similar thing happen to her. It's my theory that Anya ingested Barty's blood before they mated. As the bonding took hold, the dormant vampire blood in her system fused together the moment their souls did. I think this is what turned Anya."

"So, you think the moment Erin ingested my blood, it lay in wait until we bonded? But if that were the case, why isn't it a true mix? You said she's still human."

"I think the change will happen on her birthday."

"Like Anya," Erin says.

"Yes."

"But you can't be sure," I ask, to be clear.

"No, but I think it's the closest we've come to an actual answer."

"And yet it still comes down to us waiting," I sigh.

"Dr. Mendhi, would you give us a few minutes? Maybe you could fill in the rest of the family for us."

The moment the doctor is out of sight, Erin takes me into her arms. "Amelia, this is good news."

"It's more guesswork," I croak.

"It's not guesswork. Anya's blood is proof. My blood is proof that we are close to an answer."

"But what if we take this at face value and it doesn't play out that way on your birthday?"

"What if an asteroid falls from the sky? What if we enter World War III? Amelia, we can't answer everything, but we can sure as hell hang on to the good news we've just been given. I know it's hard and you're struggling—"

"Aren't you?" I snap.

"Yes, I am, but you're the one who gets bent out of shape because you can't control everything."

"I'm not—"

"Yes, you are. You're failing to see the positive. And, baby, that's all we have."

"We need more information," I huff. "I need to find the doctor again." For whatever reason, my brain won't allow me to accept this as a win. I know there is more we can do; more we can find to give us answers. I'm not prepared to sit on my ass and wait for three years.

Erin lets go of me and sits back. I see the look of disappointment in her eyes, but I ignore it.

What kind of mate would I be to accept a couple of blood tests as the be-all and end-all? A shitty one, and I can't abide that. Standing, I swiftly swallow the remaining bourbon. Bending down, I drop a kiss on Erin's forehead before heading out in search of the doctor.

# Twenty-Nine

I collar the doctor on his way to the bathroom. His bladder can wait a few minutes longer.

"We need to talk," I bark, directing him to the stairs. Dr. Mendhi follows me silently. I wonder if he was expecting this. "Please sit," I say, waving my hand at the single seat in the corner of my room. "There has to be more we can do."

Dr. Mendhi eyes me warily. "What do you suggest?"

"Did you ever conduct blood tests on the humans that unsuccessfully mated with vampires?"

"No."

"Why not?" Surely he thought of it.

"I'm tasked to help find a cure for the fallen—"

"And yet you failed to take their human mate into account?"

"This is the first time I have come across human and vampire blood conjoined."

"Now you know, so shouldn't you be testing their blood?"

"To what end? To satisfy your need for answers? All the humans that unsuccessfully mated with a vampire are now dead. Do you wish for me to exhume the bodies for you?"

"For me? This isn't about me," I defend.

"It absolutely is, Amelia. Even if I did what you are asking, what would it prove? It would tell us what we have just discovered. You will still have to wait for Erin to turn thirty, to be sure."

"That's not acceptable," I growl.

"Maybe not, but that's all we have. I cannot expedite the process, Amelia. We know you have bonded, that's almost a certainty. So why is waiting three years to see if Erin changes so terrible?"

"Because..." Because what? If Erin was already a vampire, we would have to wait. There is no difference. When I think of Erin changing, I feel... wrong? Something doesn't sit right about it. Is that why I want to know if it will happen? Am I scared she *will* change?

"You're conflicted," he says matter-of-factly.

"I don't want to live without her," I whisper, mostly to myself.

"But the idea of her changing is a problem?" The doctor understands me more than I like.

Gripping my hair in my hands, I stare at the floor. What's going on with me? I should be jumping for joy that Erin and I mated. But all I feel is fear and anxiety. I thought it was because I could lose Erin, or that she would reject me. But maybe it's because I might actually get to keep her. But at what cost?

"Can I give you some advice?" The doctor is sitting with his elbows on his knees, his chin resting on his fists. I nod. "Speak to Erin. And I mean, lay it all out there for her. I'm a doctor and I trust in science and what I can prove with data. But... after working with you and after talking with Barty and Anya, I believe there is more to the mating process. More than science can explain."

"Meaning?"

"The reason you and Erin didn't initially bond after being physical was because you were holding back from her. I believe that immortality isn't guaranteed for any of us."

"What are you talking about?" I laugh mirthlessly. "Of course it is. When vampire's mate, they become immortal. Everyone knows that."

"I beg to differ. We've assumed that's how it works, but I think there's more to it. I think we actively choose immortality."

"You're losing me."

"It's only now that I see the truth."

"And the truth would be?" My patience is ebbing.

"Just like the bonding process, if two people don't give themselves one hundred percent willingly, if they don't choose to be immortal, they won't."

"You think vampires can choose a different path?"

"Yes."

"What?"

"You need to forget what you think you know," he says. Because that's easy, right? "Before we were aware of the 'rules' surrounding our change, vampires simply fell in love. They weren't burdened with finding a mate before their thirtieth birthday. They found their soulmate, and that was that. Just like humans. They found their love and embraced it forever. It was their choice.

"When you finally gave yourself fully to Erin, you chose to do that, as did she." Is this what Barty meant when he said vampires could choose immortality?

"Okay, let me get this straight. You believe that Erin and I could choose not to become immortal?"

"Yes. For Erin, the consequences of that decision are unknown, but we know what that would mean for you. Although, factoring in my new theory…" I lose him momentarily to his thoughts. He's obviously working through some sort of epiphany.

"I'll go nuts." I interject.

"Maybe."

"Great!"

"Amelia. The question here is why are you fighting this so much? Is it simply because you've expected your time on Earth to end at thirty for so long that the alternative is unthinkable, or is it more?"

"I didn't know you were a Doctor of Psychology too!" I snap. Dr. Mendhi holds up his hands, mimicking his surrender.

"I have no such qualification. I'll leave you to your thoughts. Although, Amelia, I would be remiss to leave you without telling you to talk to Erin. If not her, your family. Because what's ruminating in your mind is the one thing that will put both your and Erin's immortality at risk. Of that I'm sure."

Hiding away in my room isn't helping. I keep replaying my conversation with the doctor. I know I need to talk to Erin. But before that, I need to get things straight in my mind.

What is it about Erin changing that is making me feel this way? Am I still hung up on mating with a human? After several moments of introspection, I know that's not it, but I think it does have something to do with humanity. Yes, that's it. I don't feel comfortable with Erin giving up her humanity. But then, does that mean I think vampires are less than humans? No, that doesn't track.

"Penny for your thoughts?" I close my eyes and let the melody of Erin's voice wash over me.

"I was just on my way down," I lie.

"No, you weren't. You were hiding up here. I just want to know why and how I can help?"

Holding my hand out to her, I breathe a sigh of relief when her warmth and love tingles through my body the moment her skin touches my own. "Sit," I say, squeezing her hand.

"Please tell me what's wrong, Amelia. I'm not blind. You wear your emotions on your face for the world to see."

"I had an interesting chat with Dr. Mendhi," I begin. "He now thinks we can choose immortality. That it's entirely up to us."

"That's an interesting thought."

"Hmmm."

"You don't think he's right?"

"I don't know, maybe."

"So, is that what you wanted to talk to him about? Immortality?"

"No, I wanted him to... I just wanted—"

"Wanted what? Amelia, what more could he, me, or you possibly do? We have our answer. Or is that the problem? You don't like what he said. You don't like the thought of me changing."

"Do you know what you would be choosing? I mean, really? It's okay for you to say you want this, to live with me forever, but you're human. You were meant to live and grow old with your family. They will get old and die. You will have to watch everyone you love leave. You won't even be able to be there with them in the end because, unlike them, you won't have aged a day."

"I understand that," Erin begins, but she can't possibly mean it.

"How can you say that so calmly? I couldn't watch my brothers and sisters grow old and die. Nor my parents."

"Amelia, I don't have all the answers. It's not like I saw any of this coming—"

"I know, and that makes it worse. It makes this impossible situation my fault. I should have just stayed away. I'd made peace with my future."

"You think you should have hidden away and waited to go mad? You think you should have gotten to the point where your parents or siblings had to decide which one of them would have to kill you?" Erin is getting worked up, but she isn't shouting, she isn't running. Not like me.

"But you would have been safe, Erin. You would have made a life, probably with Mack."

"Mack?"

"Yes. I know you liked her. She may have messed up in the end, but I think she's a decent person. Just a tad jealous."

"Amelia, what the hell are you going on about?"

"She still likes you; you know. I saw her at the club not so long ago. You were talking at the bar."

"Mack came to apologize and ask if she could have another chance. However, she was under no illusions once I told her how I felt about you. Why didn't you tell me you saw that?"

"I thought if it were anything important, you would tell me. Anyway, it's not about that. I want you to be happy and safe, surrounded by the people you love. Not losing them."

"I love you, Amelia, and I love your family. I'm not going to deny it will hurt when those times come, and I have to say goodbye to my parents or my friends. But that's an inevitability anyway. Death is a part of life. But Amelia, it's my choice. I'm not blindly following you like some lovesick puppy. My soul is yours, my heart and mind, too. If I thought my parents would understand, I would tell them about all of this. And I'm pretty sure they would encourage me to follow my heart."

"Your entire life will change. You'll need to drink red. Have you thought about that?"

"I doubt that will be an issue. When I change—"

"If you change."

"No, when. If Dr. Mendhi is correct, it's my choice, right? I've made peace with the new trajectory of my life, Amelia. It's time you did the same. Forget about me and what will happen. That's my burden to bear. Think about yourself and what you want. Do you want to spend eternity with me?"

"I could choose mortality," I say.

"You'd be choosing death. We know what it would mean for you to stay mortal."

"Not necessarily, according to the good doctor—"

"You're willing to gamble on a theory?"

"Isn't that what we're doing now?"

"No, it's not. We've bonded. I've tasted your blood. There is no reason to think I won't change just like Anya, unless... you decide you don't want that. I may be new to the world of vampires, Amelia, but I'm a quick study. If the doctor is right and our choice can make a difference, the only way I will remain mortal is if you choose that. Not me, I know what I want." Erin rises from the bed, still holding my hand. "Decide what you want, Amelia, for both our sakes."

"Erin—"

"No, I've said what I needed to say. No one can give you the answers you're searching for, love, no one but you."

Erin leaves me to my own thoughts, and I immediately miss her presence. Closing my eyes, I home in on her. It's wonderful knowing no matter where in the world I am, I will always feel her with me. Is that how Erin feels about me?

# Thirty

There is no choice to make. My rational brain knows that. I cannot live without Erin. And yet this panic attack I seem to be suffering from would indicate my rational brain isn't in charge of me right now.

Squeezing my eyes shut, I count my breaths, hoping they will slow enough for me to take a proper lungful of air. Why am I spiraling? A large hand on my back brings me back from the brink of unconsciousness. "Breathe, Amelia," my father's voice instructs delicately.

My eyes snap open, seeking his, and the safety they offer. I can hear my raspy breathing. My chest is tight. "I... I..."

"It's okay, honey. In and out, nice and slow. Listen to me breathing and try to follow along." He places my hand on his chest, and I can feel it rise and fall. It's working.

My body is mimicking his and my breathing is becoming steady and calm.

"Th-thank you," I stutter. I grip his shirt, anchoring myself. This is not me. I don't have panic attacks. I'm the calm child, the laid-back one, not this!

"Are you feeling up for telling me what brought this on?" he asks quietly.

"I... I don't know. Everything just feels out of control."

"Understandably," he placates. "I don't think I have ever seen you have a panic attack, though, Amelia. You're usually quite steadfast and confident in your emotions." That's right, I am. I think logically and realistically. Well, I used to do that. "Is this something to do with Dr. Mendhi's news?"

"Yes and no," I answer honestly. "He told you?" My father nods. "And it's good, right? It's a positive step."

"It is. Do you think differently?"

"No, I know it's what we've been waiting for."

"But?"

"No but. I've just been feeling overwhelmed lately."

My father settles on the bed next to me, his arm tugging me to his body. "You've always been the stoic one, you know. As a child, you would endure everything on your own, no matter how much your mother and I wanted to help. You had to do it alone."

I wipe my face free of tears and look at his face again. I'm so similar to him in every way. "I enjoy working things out on my own," I reply. I've never meant to cut my parents out, or my other siblings. It's just how I operate.

"I know, honey. It's not a bad thing."

"But?" I smile, which he returns.

"But I think it means you've never fully allowed yourself to let someone else in. I don't know why you guarded your little heart so fiercely back then and now, but I think that's what drives you to keep to yourself."

Looking back, I remember feeling uncomfortable anytime I was vulnerable. There is no specific memory I have of the reason I felt the need to shy away from others. All I know is that it felt safer that way.

"Having the ability to shield yourself like that is probably why you handled not finding a mate better than all of us combined," he smiles. "But you are still a person with emotions. Recent events have been hard on all of us, but especially you, sweetie."

"Why, though, why can't I deal with it like I normally do?"

"Because you've never let anyone close enough until Erin. Now you have a whole other person to worry about and I think that terrifies you."

It does. Before Erin, I never felt the urge to protect someone with my life. Of course, I love my family, but it's not the same. Maybe that's why I didn't do much to find a mate? My mind knew I wouldn't be able to cope with all the uncertainty having a mate entails. I can't control the world; therefore I can't keep Erin safe. And that's all I want to do. The thought of anything happening to that perfect specimen of a human being claws at my heart. I feel the vice grip of worry clamp down on me again at the mere thought of Erin not being okay. I can handle something happening to me, but not her.

"Your worry and your need for answers are just a reaction to feeling something foreign. It will pass, Amelia, if you let Erin help you. It's not on you to be the strong one all of the time."

"But I need to be strong. I need to do what's best for Erin."

"And what is it you think is best?"

"I... I told her it might have been better if she'd never met me. If she'd stayed with Mack." I sob at the thought of Erin with someone other than me.

"Do you really believe what you said?"

I shake my head. "No," I whisper.

"I can't imagine it felt good for Erin to hear you say those things."

"What about when she has to say goodbye to her family?" I ask. My brain will just *not* let go of all the insecurities whirling around my body.

"You will get through it together. I know this is scary, Amelia. I know you want to push everything and everyone away because you think that's what will keep you safe, but you're wrong. Life is uncertain. There are no guarantees, but if you choose to push Erin away, you are guaranteeing her pain and your own."

"I never want to hurt her."

"Then stop running from her. Stop demanding answers and control. Be here, with her, through it all. Be her mate, the one she deserves, the one she fell in love with."

Wrapping my arms around my father, I hold him tight. "Thank you."

"Anytime, sweetie. That's what I'm here for."

"I can't believe you're going to be a daddy again," I laugh through my tears. Whatever I'm going through, I feel it might be coming to an end. I just hope Erin will forgive me. I'm clearly not going to be an easy vampire to love. Who knew I had so many unknown issues I need to work through?

"Another Loch," he laughs. "It's going to be fun."

"I hope we have that someday."

"A child?"

"Yeah. One that looks like Erin. Gold hair and blue eyes. There's enough lanky raven-haired vampires in this family already," I chuckle.

"So I'm carrying our kid now?" Erin is standing in the hallway, smiling at me.

"I'll leave you two to talk," Father whispers. He passes Erin and kisses her on the cheek.

"Hey," I say weakly.

"I was eavesdropping," Erin states boldly. Should I be mad? I'm not, if anything, I'm relieved. "You've been holding a lot inside, my love, for a very long time, by the sounds of it."

"I didn't know I was the type to have a breakdown," I smile shyly.

"Have you really been this scared all along?" Erin kneels in front of me, her chin rests on my lap as she looks up into my eyes.

"I have never felt this way about anything or anyone, Erin. All the uncertainty just got too much. I've finally found you, and so far, everything has pointed to me losing you. It's painful to even contemplate."

"I know the feeling, sweetie. The moment I learned what could happen to you if we didn't mate was the worst thing I think I've ever had to hear."

"But we mated. I'm not going to fall."

"If you choose us, no, you won't. Are you ready to do that? Face your fears and be with me? No matter what the outcome is on my birthday?"

Nodding, I take her face in my hands, gently urging her to her feet. Looking up into her angelic face, I know I have to stop letting my anxiety and negativity win. "I'll be with you every step of the way. I choose you, Erin, always. I choose immortality with you, if that's what you want. I'll do anything for you, my love."

"Anything?"

"Anything!"

"Make love to me, Amelia."

There is nothing on this Earth I want more. I've been foolish, pushing Erin away when I know she is the only person in my life that can anchor me, make me believe everything will work out, that we really can have eternity together.

I remain sitting on the end of the bed. Opening my legs, I urge her to step between them. My hands gently grip her waist as I take her in. She is exquisite, and she is mine. Erin runs her hands through my hair, which sends tingles throughout my entire body. "Kiss me," I whisper.

Bending forward, Erin brushes her nose against mine. I hear her inhale deeply. Her grip tightens on my head, causing electricity to bolt through my pussy. God, I want her. Instead of our lips meeting, Erin swipes her tongue across my bottom lip faintly. I respond by dropping my hands to her ass, pulling her forward until she's straddling my legs.

With her dress bunched up around her thighs, I massage her backside, encouraging her to move those sensual hips. Erin's pillowy lips find my neck. I feel the tip of her tongue against my skin and then a delicious pain as she bites down.

Twisting my body, I flip us 'round. Erin lands on her back with a soft bounce. Releasing my grip, I push her dress up higher and then I see she's gone commando and all my birthdays and Christmases have been made. "You're not wearing any panties," I growl, my mouth salivating at her pink, swollen folds.

"Nope," she states, and her eyes flash with need.

"You are perfect, Erin Hanson," I mutter, already lowering my head. The first taste of her sweet ambrosia makes my eyes retreat to the back of my skull. She's like fine wine.

Her clit is rigid. If I close my eyes and focus, I can almost hear the blood pulsing through it. I can feel its desperate cry for attention. My tongue traces the edge of her desire. Erin shivers and groans. Her hands grip the duvet hard.

"Amelia, suck me, please."

Her pleas obliterate my restraint. Surging forward, I take her clit into my mouth. Her hips move with every slow suck and together we form a rhythm that is moving Erin closer to exultation. My hands travel up her torso. I blindly pull at the cups of her strapless dress. My fingertips meet her supple breasts. I palm them, massaging, then pulling her nipples, all the time amping up the tempo of my sucks and licks.

"Yes," she hisses, as I pinch her nipples a little harder. I am completely in tune with her body. I can feel the exact moment my actions breathe life into her building pleasure.

Opening my eyes, I am stunned to see waves of light radiating off Erin. Gold and blue hues pulse and she shakes. "Oh... oh, Amelia... I'm... I'm com—" Her voice cuts off abruptly as her orgasm rips through her body. I continue sucking until Erin's hand on my head begs me to stop. "I... I can't take it anymore."

My face is covered in her come, and I want more. Sliding up her body, I rest myself on top of her. Our kiss is fierce, but full of love. Erin cleans my mouth with her tongue. I reach between her legs and enter her. I love the way I steal her breath and the way she bites my chin.

Her hands fumble with the clasp of my pants. Moving, I create space for Erin's fingers to slide into my panties. I know I'm dripping, and Erin's little pleasurable groan tells me she's just as happy as I am that her fingers are being coated with my arousal.

Our tongues and teeth clash as we fuck each other. Erin wanted me to make love to her, and I am, but I can't go slow, not right now. My carnal desire to ravage her is too strong. Although, with the way Erin is pumping into me, I don't think she could slow down either.

"Er—Erin," I grunt, my hips pushing her fingers deeper and I am about to explode. "Fuck, yes!" I gasp as I flood her hand. Those blue and gold hues dance in front of my eyes once again. Our collective screams are swallowed by each other.

Rolling off her, I take Erin into my arms. Her head snuggles into my neck, and we simply lay there, recovering. Minutes pass before Erin stirs. "Did you see that?" she asks. My mind is still in a sex haze, and I don't really understand what she's saying. "Did you see the colors?"

I shift my head to see her better. "Yes, I saw. I saw them when we mated as well."

"I think that's all the proof you need, my love, that we are made for each other. We literally create beauty together."

"I'll never question us ever again. I swear it."

# Epilogue

Today is my thirtieth birthday. At the stroke of midnight, I'll become immortal. Sounds like a fairytale, doesn't it? But I assure you it's real. This year has tested me in ways I never believed possible.

After finally talking through all my fears with Erin all those months ago, I vowed to myself I would never let my fears and insecurities get to me like that again. It's been a process, let me tell you. I spend a lot of time practicing mindfulness and yoga.

Whenever I feel that fear creeping back into my mind, I bend myself like a pretzel for an hour whilst listening to ocean sounds. I've never felt more Zen, and I have Erin to thank for that. She has been my rock and greatest supporter. However, to her chagrin, she still hasn't gotten me to where I can spend more than an hour with Lucille without wanting to commit homicide. What can I say? I'm a work in progress.

So, instead of worrying myself to death, I spent this last year getting to know my mate. Although our souls are bonded for all eternity, we became a couple extremely fast, even by lesbian standards—as my mother likes to joke.

Erin deserved—and still does—to be wined and dined. We went on a second first date—without the piercing pain of my suffering soul, this time. On the third date, Erin did in fact put out (again) to my utter delight. Everything with her has been so easy.

We still have two years until Erin hits The Big 3-0. I can't deny it hovers at the back of my mind most days. All signs point to Erin changing, but there is no guarantee.

Unlike last year, I am not woken by my brother Laurence but by Erin's tongue sucking on my nipple. I've tried to pretend I'm still sleeping, but the moment she clamps down, just the way I like it, my body betrays me, and I let out a small gasp.

"I knew you were awake," Erin mumbles, my stiff bud still in her mouth.

"I didn't want to distract you," I reply, my hand making its way to her hair. The sun is shining through the open double windows. The ocean air gently wafting over our warm bodies.

"You couldn't distract me from this if you tried," she adds, swapping to my other breast.

Closing my eyes, I bask in the sensations Erin is eliciting with her tongue. All too suddenly, that sensational appendage disappears, forcing me to open my eyes. Erin is leaning over the side of the bed, rifling through her open luggage.

Propping myself up on my elbows, I smile because I have a fantastic view of Erin's bare ass. Oh, it's just dying to be spanked. "None of that," Erin says, her head still dangling over the side of our king-size four-poster bed.

"What, I didn't do anything," I reply, feigning innocence.

"I could hear your thoughts, Amelia. There will be time for spanking later. First, you need to open your birthday present."

"Well, if you insist," I joke.

"This is your first present. The one only I can see," she winks, upping my excitement by a million. I take the wrapped box out of her hand and tear into it. Erin has bought us a double-ended dildo.

"Happy birthday to me," I grin, taking my new toy out of its packaging.

"Let me go wash it. Why don't you start without me?"

I hate to burst Erin's bubble, but there's nothing for me to start. I've been wet from the second she touched her lips to my skin.

Erin strolls to the ensuite, her naked body on show in all its small wonder. Jesus, her ass is to die for. While she cleans the dildo, I stretch my body, still a little sore from our lovemaking last night. My mind wanders to the day ahead, but I'm not in my thoughts for long. The bed dips as Erin rejoins me.

"Open up, baby," she says, her hands already spreading my legs.

"I want you on top," I say.

Erin rubs the small end of the dildo through my lips. I love to see the grin that spreads across her face when she sees how much I want her. "How does that feel?" she asks as she pushes it inside me.

"Perfect. Now it's your turn."

Pushing herself up slowly, Erin climbs over me, her pussy hovering just above the tip of the toy. "Give it to me hard," she says before lowering herself down. I watch spellbound as the toy slowly disappears inside my mate. Her hand reaches between us and suddenly the entire thing vibrates, causing my head to sink into the pillow. "Oh God," I moan.

Erin's hands land on my stomach as she lifts herself up and down. I get a grip on my libido, forcing myself to hold back. Taking Erin by the hips, I thrust in time with her movement. I'm not sure either of us will last long. The pleasure is outstanding.

"Harder," she cries. I'm biting my lip so hard; I must be drawing blood. Flipping us over, I pound into Erin with everything I have. Her hands reach above her head, gripping the headboard. "Yes, yes, like that, oh fuck."

I drop my head slightly as I fight to keep my orgasm at bay until Erin is ready. "Erin," I gasp because I am losing the battle. I feel my walls clamp around the toy and those familiar blue and gold colors swim in front of my eyes.

"I'm coming, I'm coming," she groans, and my walls break, allowing the climax to surge over my entire body. I feel our energies merge. I feel Erin's soul dance with my own as we tumble together.

"Wow!" is the only word I can conjure in the aftermath. I pull out of Erin slowly and then remove it from myself. Dropping the dildo to the bed, I roll off Erin and starfish. I am completely spent.

"Incredible," she mumbles into my neck as she curls her body around mine.

"Can we stay here all day?" I ask, semi-seriously.

"You know we have to meet the family at lunch."

"But do we? *Really*?"

"Not unless you want Lucille breaking the door down. Or your mother."

"Are you still glad they joined us on this trip?"

"Yes, I am. It's not like we're sharing a room with them. We have a suite all to ourselves."

"Yes, but when mother gifted me the trip to Hawaii last year, I didn't realize that I had to bring them along."

"Do you need five minutes of meditation before we venture out?"

Erin might have been joking, but yes, that's exactly what I need. So far we have been in Hawaii for three days, and we have spent every single one of those with my family.

"You know they just want to support you, honey. Especially today. It's been a long road for us all."

"I know," I sigh. "I'll be fine. Let me have a few minutes on the balcony to center myself and then we'll get ready."

The sun is blazing over Kauai. There isn't a single cloud in the sky. I take deep breaths, focusing on the sounds of nature. It doesn't take me long to reset and feel peace.

Erin's arm snakes around my torso. She holds me close, her head resting on my back. "I love you."

"I love you, too."

"I'm exhausted. Can we please go back to the suite?" I mutter under my breath to Erin.

"Amelia, we can't. Not until after midnight. They need to be here for you."

"Why, nothing is actually going to happen. They can't actually see the change begin."

"It doesn't matter. Let them have this, and then you can have me in whatever position you want."

"Alright then."

Erin titters. "That didn't take a whole lot of convincing, my love."

"I'm not stupid," I grin.

Our conversation is interrupted by my father rising from his seat. We've been sitting in my parents' bungalow for hours, eating and drinking. "Can I have your attention please?" he asks. "Shut it," he barks at Lucille, who is yammering away at Trent about something. "Thank you. Now, the time is almost upon us. Two minutes until Amelia sheds her mortal skin."

"Jesus, Father, that's a bit much," Jacob laughs.

"Yes, I heard it," Father chuckles. "In all seriousness. Amelia, this day has felt like a long time coming, but has also arrived far too fast. We're proud of you, sweetheart." I tip my glass in his direction.

"Get ready," my mother calls. Naturally, my eyes drift to the big clock on the wall. My heart rate rises in anticipation. Even though I know I won't fall into madness, there is still a sliver of fear.

I watch as the seconds tick by. Three... Two... One. I close my eyes and hold my breath. A small quiver passes over my heart and then it's gone.

Opening my eyes, I laugh when I see dozens of eyes trained on me. I weigh up putting on a show, pretending something is happening, but then I come to my senses. Mother might actually kill me if I make fun. Erin's hand caresses my thigh. I smile at her sweetly.

"I'm okay," I say to her.

"I know," she replies. My family are hugging each other and laughing with abandon. They really were stressed.

Hawaiian dancers enter the room. A surprise my parents have cooked up, I bet. Music begins and a fresh round of drinks is poured. Reaching into my pocket, I pull out the ring box I've been carrying for six months. I wanted to ask Erin to marry me when I bought it, but I knew I had to wait until my rebirth. That's what I'm calling it.

Erin is smiling at the dancers. I'm smiling at her. I see my mother in the corner of my eye jab my father in the ribs. She's spotted the ring box on the table. Trailing my fingers down Erin's cheek, I wait for her to turn. Her eyes zero in on the box and then go wide, making me chuckle. "What's that?" she asks.

"That's a ring," I reply. "A ring I hope you will agree to wear."

"A ring?"

I don't think I've ever seen Erin lost for words. "Yes, a ring. We are bound in body and mind, Erin, but I want to be bound to you by law. Erin Hanson, will you be my wife?"

Her eyes haven't left the ring box. I take it and open it gently. The sapphire is the same color as her eyes. I knew it belonged to Erin the second I saw it. Taking the ring from its cushion, I push back my chair and drop to both knees. "I will cherish you always. I will protect you with all that I have, and I will love you until my last breath. Erin, marry me."

Her finger slips through the ring, but she still hasn't said anything. Her eyes slowly make their way to mine. I see her, all of her, and she sees me. I can hear her innermost thoughts and feel the pure joy coursing through her body.

"Yes."

We embrace as our family and even the dancers cheer. It's a perfect ending to a tumultuous year, but I need to remain vigilant. Our worries are not over until Erin turns. Waiting for eternity will be a test for us all.

Amelia and Erin's journey continues in *Waiting For Eternity*.
Out January 2025

# Thank you!

Save and author by leaving a review. Just a few words can
help an indie author reach more readers.

Amazon

Goodreads

# Other Titles By Alyson Root

# Acknowledgements

*I'll keep this brief. To my friends, K and C, thank you for your constant support. To Tara for being a fantastic editor. And to my wife for being my constant. I love you.*

# About the author

Alyson was born and raised in the heart of England. She moved to Paris in 2015 when she met her wife. Together they moved to the west of France where they now live with their two dogs. Alyson spends her time reading lesbian romance books, writing and Scuba Dive.

Alyson discovered her love of writing in her mid-thirties. Her debut book, *A Dance Towards Forever* was inspired by her wife and their very own love story. Alyson wrote *Diving Into Her* and *Always Emilie*, which added with her first book created The French Connection series.

www.alysonroot.com

alyson.root@outlook.com

@alyson_root

Made in the USA
Columbia, SC
30 November 2024

48027726R00183